MY MOTHER
THE MAYOR,
MAYBE

**Other APPLE PAPERBACKS
You Will Want To Read**

Casey and the Great Idea
   by Joan Lowery Nixon
The Cybil War
   by Betsy Byars
Dreams of Victory
   by Ellen Conford
The Girl with the Silver Eyes
   by Willo Davis Roberts
The Hocus-Pocus Dilemma
   by Pat Kibbe
Kid Power
   by Susan Beth Pfeffer
Nothing's Fair in Fifth Grade
   by Barthe DeClements
With a Wave of the Wand
   by Mark Jonathan Harris
Yours Till Niagara Falls, Abby
   by Jane O'Connor

MY MOTHER THE MAYOR, MAYBE

by
PAT KIBBE

Drawings by
Charles Robinson

AN
APPLE
PAPERBACK

SCHOLASTIC BOOK SERVICES
New York Toronto London Auckland Sydney Tokyo

ISBN 0-590-32654-6

12 11 10 9 8 7 6 5 4 3 2 1   9   2 3 4 5 6/8
Printed in the U.S.A.   11

For my husband,
JACK,
who really ran — and won

MY MOTHER THE MAYOR, MAYBE

Mom's Scrapbook

I THOUGHT THIS cartoon would be good pasted right on the first page of my scrapbook. **Mrs. Pinkerton is running for Mayor**—that's what the caption says, in case you can't read it. It's a little smudgy where the paste is still wet. After the election in November, when this scrapbook is full of clippings and campaign stuff, I'm going to surprise Mom and give it to her.

A cartoon is supposed to be funny, so I guess it's all right that Mom looks so silly running after Mayor Quinn and trying to catch on to his coattails. Those five kids hanging on to Mom's apron strings are supposed to be my three brothers, my sister, and me. And that man in the corner with the briefcase, looking at all of us and grinning, is Dad.

My friend Nancy Tyler says a Republican probably drew the picture because the mayor is a Republican and he looks so much better than my mother does. Mom's a Democrat—and she's beautiful, intelligent, and just what this town of Cranberry Falls needs, Dad says. She isn't at all skinny, like that cartoon shows her, and her nose isn't that big, either.

It *does* look like Mayor Quinn she's chasing. He's got a bushy head of hair and a potbelly, just the way it is in the picture.

I didn't think it was fair to print a cartoon like that. But Mom laughed when she saw it. Luckily she's got a good sense of humor. And that's very important if you're going to be in politics.

Dad says Mom's running for mayor is going to be a wonderful experience for the whole family. All we have to do is remain cool, calm, and collected—and not let anything or anybody bother us, no matter what.

So how come I'm already a nervous wreck?

Mrs Pinkerton is running for Mayor

★ ★ 1 ★ ★

Mrs. Pinkerton Is
Running for Mayor

I STARTED BEING a nervous wreck the first Thursday in September when Tony Spano threw the evening newspaper over our white picket fence. He's too lazy to come up the driveway. He pedaled past the gate and yelled, "Your old lady hasn't got a chance, B.J."

"That's what you think, stupid," I yelled back. I would have thrown a tomato or something at him, but the whole family was waiting inside to see the newspaper so I didn't have time. I also didn't have a tomato. I can't stand that Tony Spano.

Dad spread the paper out on the dining room table in front of Mom. We all crowded around and read the headline out loud like a chorus:

" 'Democrats choose woman candidate. Dorothy Pinkerton will run for mayor.' "

"Yea, Mom!" my three brothers hollered together.

"Imagine, my mother the mayor," swooned my sister, Allison.

"Maybe," I added.

"Here's a picture of the whole family," said Dad.

"Where? Let's see." Allison was so excited she practically climbed up on the table. "Oh, no," she wailed. "You can't even see my face. What's that in front of it?"

"Willie's tail," I told her. "He was so excited he was wagging it, remember?"

"Will you two girls move over so somebody else can see?" My oldest brother, Kyle, pushed in between Allison and me and began reading what it said under the picture.

" 'Smiling above, and surrounded by her happy family, is the new Democratic candidate for mayor, Dorothy Pinkerton. Standing directly behind her are her husband, attorney Jack Pinkerton, and their three sons, Kyle, 16, Jon, 14, and Ethan, 13. Seated on the sofa with Mrs. Pinkerton and Willie, the family

Democrats Choose Woman Candidate. Dorothy Pinkerton Will Run For Mayor

dog, are daughters Allison, 12, and Justine, 10.' "

"Justine? Oh, no," I moaned. "Why didn't they just put B.J.?"

"Because you wouldn't tell them the B.J. stood for Baby Justine," snickered Allison.

Before I could poke her, Kyle picked up the paper. "This happy family looks pretty sad, if you ask me. I don't even have a head."

"You're too tall," I told him. "It barely got in the picture."

"And my teeth are blacked out," said Jon.

Ethan grabbed the paper. "It's B.J.'s hair ribbon. It looks like you're eating it, Jon. Gosh, what a picture. Nobody looks human except Willie." Ethan grinned. "And he's a dog!"

"Some joke!" Jon took the paper. "Quiet, everybody. 'Democrats breathed a sigh of relief today when they announced to the *Courier* that Dorothy Pinkerton will be their new candidate for mayor. She will replace Democrat Charlie Knots, who had to quit the race because of ill health. Mrs. Pinkerton will be running against the Republicans' number one vote getter, Myron Quinn. When asked if she thought she had a chance to unseat the man who has been mayor for eighteen years, Mrs. Pinkerton was optimistic. "It's time for a change," she said. "It's time for a

Democrat to be mayor and it's time for a woman." ' "
Jon threw the newspaper up in the air. "Hooray for
Mom!"

"Yea, yea, Mom!" We all applauded and danced
around like crazy. "Speech, speech."

Dad lifted up Mom and set her right on top of the
dining room table.

As soon as she could stop laughing, she spoke.
"Thank you all for your support and confidence. I
promise to fight a hard campaign. Fortunately, it will
be a short one, eight weeks, and I promise to return
to my role of wife and mother the day after the
election."

"What do you mean?" I asked her. "Don't you
think you're going to win?"

"Of course she's going to win, B.J.," said Allison.
"Imagine, I'll be the mayor's daughter. I can get off
the school bus at Town Hall!"

"Oh, Allison." Mom laughed some more and
hopped down off the table. "I really haven't much of
a chance. There hasn't been a Democrat in office in
thirty years."

"Why not?" asked Allison.

"Because everyone in town is a Republican," Kyle
said.

"But, if you're the only Democrat and you think

you haven't got a chance, Mom," I said, "why are you running?"

"Nobody else would, B.J."

"Somebody has to keep the two-party system alive," broke in Jon. "Besides, it's an honor to be asked to run."

"Did they ask you, Dad?" said Ethan.

"Yes, but politics isn't for me. Your mother will be perfect for the job. Her father used to be in politics."

"He ran for Congress," Mom said. "And he always said every citizen should devote some time of his life to public service."

"And this is your mother's time!" Dad gave Mom a big hug.

Allison picked up the newspaper and put it back on the table. We all looked at the picture again.

"Doesn't your mother look pretty?" asked Dad.

"Yup." I pointed to the picture below. "She's prettier than Mayor Quinn."

Jon laughed. "Yeah, will you look at his hair!"

"It looks like a bush," said Ethan.

Mom turned the page. "I wish they'd mentioned that I majored in political science and went to town meetings. And I can't find a thing about the kickoff party."

"What's a kickoff party?" I asked.

"The beginning of the campaign," said Dad.

"Sure," said Kyle, "like the kickoff is the beginning of a football game."

"Wait," said Dad. "There it is, Dorothy. See? In the Coming Events column. It says the public is invited to attend a kickoff party at the Pinkertons' home this Friday."

"A party for the whole town? *Here?*" screeched Allison.

"What will you give them all to eat, Mom?" asked Jon.

"The committeemen are bringing hot dogs."

"Hot dog!" said Ethan. "My favorite."

The telephone rang.

"It's probably the League of Women Voters," said Dad. "They want you to speak at their meeting this evening."

Mom hurried out to the hall. "What can I say, Jack? I don't even have an issue to talk about."

Before I could ask Dad what an issue was, he took the newspaper and followed Mom upstairs.

The telephone was still ringing. Willie was barking at it in the kitchen.

"Isn't it wonderful?" Allison said to the boys and me. "We're going to be famous, like the Kennedys."

The front doorbell began ringing, too.

"That's probably a reporter." Allison peeked out the dining room window. "I really should fix my hair."

"Just answer the door," I told her.

"Somebody get that phone," Dad yelled down the stairs.

I raced into the kitchen. Willie was growling and turning around in circles near the desk where the telephone is. He gets very upset when there's a lot of noise.

"Somebody hold Willie," I said.

"Not me, I'm getting out of here." Jon headed for the back door.

"Me, too." Ethan ran after him.

"Wait a minute, you guys." Kyle took a pile of signs off the counter. "We have to hang these on the picket fence for Mom."

I grabbed the receiver. "Hello, hello."

Darn it. I was too late. No one was there.

Allison walked into the kitchen loaded with boxes. "It wasn't a reporter at all. It was Marianne Spano delivering Girl Scout cookies. Who was on the phone?"

"I don't know."

"Were you disconnected?"

I looked down. Willie had chewed the telephone

wire right off the wall. "I was disconnected all right. Did you tell Marianne to come to the kickoff party tomorrow?"

"The Spanos can't come."

"I thought they were going to help with Mom's campaign."

"They're not on our side anymore."

"What do you mean?"

"Mr. Spano's been made campaign manager for Mayor Quinn."

"What?" I couldn't believe it. "But Mayor Quinn's a Republican! Tony Spano said they were Democrats!"

"I know. It's awful." Allison opened one of the boxes and stuffed a cookie in her mouth. "If your own neighbors aren't for you, who is?"

Mom rushed down the back stairs with the newspaper and hurried to the phone. "Your father convinced me I should speak to the League of Women Voters tonight. I'm going to call the *Courier* to see if they'll send a reporter to cover the meeting. It would be good publicity."

"It's out of order," I said.

"What?"

"The telephone. Willie ate it."

Mom pulled Willie out from under the desk. I was hoping she'd whack him with the newspaper. Instead, she patted him like he was a baby. No wonder he's spoiled!

"I'll walk down to the Spanos'," Mom said. "I have to call the telephone company anyway. We're going to need another phone."

"What for? We already have two."

Mom didn't answer me. She was out the door and on her way down the hill.

"Don't go to the Spanos'," I hollered. "That's enemy territory."

She didn't hear me, or didn't care. Neither did Willie. He trotted right after her.

"Willie isn't going to like it with so much going on and Mom so busy." I picked up the newspaper and looked at it again.

"Don't worry. He'll survive," Dad said, coming down the back stairs. "Now, let's set the table."

I nearly fainted because my father never set the table before in his life. He never even cleared it.

The boys came running in. They were out of breath and they were furious. They'd nailed the kickoff party signs all around the fence. When they went back to see how they looked, somebody had already pulled them off.

"Who would do a thing like that?" asked Dad.

"A Republican," said Allison.

"Tony Spano," I said. I can't stand that Tony Spano.

After dinner, Mom went to speak at the meeting and Dad went to night court.

Allison turned on the television set.

"You're not supposed to watch," Jon told her. "Do your homework."

"There might be something on the news about Mom," she said.

"Don't be ridiculous," said Kyle. "Why would there be anything on the national network about Mom running for mayor in a small town like Cranberry Falls?"

"Because she's a woman," said Allison.

"And the only Democrat in town," I added.

"If she wins, maybe she'll get on a show like 'That's Incredible,'" joked Ethan.

Allison got angry. "That's not even funny, Ethan."

I didn't say anything. While we watched the news, I cut both pictures—the one of our family and the one of Mayor Quinn—out of the paper for my scrapbook. I kept trying to figure out how Mom could get enough votes to win if everyone in town was a Republican. I finally asked Kyle.

"You don't have to vote Republican just because you're registered that way. You can change your mind and vote for a Democrat, like Mom."

"And that's what they're going to do, B.J.," Allison said. "Mom is going to win. And in January, she'll be inaugurated just like the President. We'll all get dressed up and go to Town Hall and our pictures will be on the very front page of the *Courier*."

"She could lose," said Ethan.

"What do you think, Jon?" I knew Jon probably had it all figured out. He's a mathematical genius.

Jon stood up in front of the television set and started acting like he was an announcer or something. "Ladies and gentlemen: In the tiny Republican hamlet of Cranberry Falls, the race for mayor is going to be very close. And I predict that Mrs. Pinkerton will win—"

"Hooray!" shouted Allison.

"—or lose," he continued, "by a hair." Jon gave her a silly look.

Allison threw a pillow and hit him smack in the face. "That's a stupid statement. If a race is that close, it'll be a tie."

I looked again at the pictures I'd cut out of the paper.

"I wish Mom didn't have that permanent," I told Allison. "Her hair looks bushy, like Mayor Quinn's."

"Why, B.J. Pinkerton. What a thing to say. Mom

looks perfect. Short, curly hair is 'in' this year. Besides, that's not important at all."

But it was important. And it's funny how I knew, even then, that Mom would win or lose by a hair, like Jon said.

★ ★ 2 ★ ★
Dog Eats Dog at Kickoff Party

THE NEXT DAY in social studies, Mr. Shattelles congratulated me in front of the whole class because Mom was running for mayor. That made me feel really good. But then he congratulated Tony Spano because his father was campaign manager for Mayor Quinn. I began to feel sick.

Mr. Shattelles said he had a terrific idea. "In a few weeks, why don't we let Tony and B.J. have a debate over the issues?"

Boy, did I feel sick!

Tony didn't think it was such a good idea either,

ɔecause when the class voted on whether or not we'd have a debate, we lost, twenty to two.

Just before the bell rang, Mr. Shattelles announced that our homework assignment for the next two months would be to get involved in local politics. The whole class groaned and looked at me as if it were my fault.

"You mean we have to take sides?" some kid asked.

"Well, there are two main political parties, the Republicans and the Democrats."

"Which one do you belong to, Mr. Shattelles?" the girl in front of me asked.

He smiled. "I vote for the man, not the party."

That jerk Tony Spano piped up. "You must be a Republican then, because Mrs. Pinkerton's a *woo*-man."

The class groaned again.

"Let's remember we're in the fifth grade and not kindergarten." Mr. Shattelles straightened his neck-tie. "For your weekend homework, read the *Courier* and get acquainted with the issues."

My best friend, Nancy Tyler, raised her hand. "My mother donated the mustard for the Democrats' kickoff party tonight. Can I use that as my home-work?"

"Only if you go and take notes." Mr. Shattelles looked over at the clock.

"Hey," that smart-aleck Tony piped up again. "That makes *three* parties—Republicans, Democrats, and Kickoffs."

Thank goodness the bell rang.

I always sit with Nancy on the school bus. We sit in the very front seat behind Mike Callahan, our bus driver. It's more private. It's also the farthest we can get from Tony Spano, who sits in the back and throws spitballs at everybody. He doesn't dare throw anything at us because he might get Mr. Callahan instead. Allison sits near the back too, with Amy Walker. They were put there because they talk too much and it disturbs Mike. You could still hear them though, and Allison was inviting everyone to the kickoff party.

Nancy and I were talking about the debate. I told her if it was the last thing I did, I was going to beat the pants off Tony Spano.

"Good," she said. "And I'll help you. I'd like to help your mother too, but I can't come to the kickoff party. I'm going to the movies."

"That's okay."

Nancy sighed. "But it's a rough game."

"Huh?"

"Politics. My parents said it's a rough game. They wondered why a nice person like your mother wasn't a Republican."

"Because she's a Democrat. What's the difference anyway?"

"None, I guess. But on top of that, she's a woman."

"So what?"

"It's a terrible combination. Especially in a hick town like Cranberry Falls. And did you see that television show the other night? This man was running for governor. You wouldn't believe what the bad guys did to get rid of him. I can't imagine what they would have done to him if he'd been a woman, like your mother."

The bus stopped.

"You watch too much television, Nancy," I told her.

"You getting off?" Mike was looking at us in the mirror.

Nancy stood up. "But don't worry. I'll help you win the you know what." She hopped off the bus.

"Thanks for the mustard," I hollered out the window. That Nancy's crazy sometimes, but she's a good friend.

I started worrying about the debate, even though Nancy said she'd help me. I decided as soon as I got home I'd ask Mom what Mr. Shattelles and everyone meant by "issues."

Mike stopped the bus in front of our house and said how nice the place looked. The kickoff signs were back on the fence, and the boys were putting huge goal posts at the driveway entrance.

As I ran toward the house, Allison raced past me. I thought she was headed for the barn. Instead, she went down to the lower field.

"I'm going to put Love in her stall," she yelled. "The poor thing might get nervous with strangers roaming around."

The truth is, Allison's afraid some kid might ask for a ride. And she's so stingy, she won't let anyone even look at her old horse.

Dad was in the kitchen. He must have come home early from the office to help.

"Where's Mom?" I asked.

"Upstairs practicing her speech."

I figured I'd better wait and learn about the issues at the kickoff party.

What a party. The only people who came were the Democratic candidates and their families. The only thing "kicked off" was Willie. Every time he tried to swipe a hot dog from the tray, somebody kicked him off the terrace.

I was in the keeping room. It's really a family

room, but Mom calls it the keeping room because we live in what used to be an old farmhouse. There's not much property because they built new houses all around us, but at least they left the barn and the lower field.

Anyway, I was sitting on the window seat waiting for the crowds to arrive so I could take out the ice and the punch bowl. Mom and the others were waiting too. I could see them through the window, standing on the terrace ready to give their speeches. Jon was checking the microphone and amplifier Kyle had borrowed from the Mudheads. They're a rock group. Kyle plays the drums for them.

Jon leaned toward the mike. "Testing. One, two, testing. . . ." It "tested" so loud that even inside I had to cover my ears. Willie couldn't stand it either. I watched him swipe another hot dog and run for the barn.

Ethan squashed his nose against the window pane and motioned for me to come out.

At the doorway, Dad took the punch bowl and handed me the hot dog tray. "Be sure Cyrilla Cornsby gets one, B.J."

Cyrilla Cornsby's a reporter. She writes mostly for the society column, but Allison says Cyrilla is always at everything in town, trying to get a big scoop so the *Courier* will promote her. I could see her at the other end of the terrace talking to the candidates. The feathers in her hat made her look like some sort of bird flying around taking pictures. Mom's campaign manager, Sam Jessup, was smoking a big cigar and doing most of the talking. Allison was running all over the place passing out paper napkins. I could tell by the way she kept grinning at Cyrilla, she was counting on getting her picture in the newspaper again. Instead, they printed a picture of Willie. It says, **Dog Eats Dog at Kickoff Party.** I put it in my scrapbook.

Finally, when everybody realized nobody was coming, Mr. Jessup decided to introduce the candidates anyway.

I stood with the boys near the amplifier and microphone.

"It looks like the Democrats scraped the bottom of the barrel," muttered Kyle.

"Except for Mom," said Ethan.

I agreed, especially when the man who was running for highway supervisor got up to make his speech. He was so nervous he couldn't remember his own name.

"My name is—uh—my name is uh—" he mumbled into the microphone.

Dog Eats Dog At Kickoff Party

"Tom Crawford," Jon whispered to him.

"Tom Crawford," he repeated.

His speech was okay after that. Only trouble was, his name wasn't Tom Crawford. It was Joe Belluci. Tom Crawford was running for councilman.

Mom's speech wasn't so good either. All she talked about was making a touchdown. And she's never even played football. Ethan said it was the perfect speech because after all it *was* a kickoff party. But I think it sounded dumb. I wondered why she just didn't mention how she was going to beat Mayor Quinn.

After they left, we had to take down the goal posts and remove the signs from the fence.

"At least there's not much to clean up," said Allison.

"What'll I do with this, Mom?" I pointed to a huge carton in the middle of the floor.

"Oh, dear, the committeemen forgot their hot dogs."

I looked inside the box. "There must be hundreds left over."

"We'll put them in the freezer."

"You mean, we get to keep them?" asked Ethan.

"They'll be used during the campaign. And the official opening of headquarters is next Saturday. We'll need some then."

"You mean they found a place, Dorothy?" said Dad. "That's good. Where's it going to be?"

"Opposite the Republican headquarters on Main Street. We're going to use the abandoned railroad station."

"*Yuk*," said Allison. "Nobody's been near that old dump for years. Why couldn't the Democrats get a better place?"

"Because no one would rent them one. Cranberry Falls is a Republican town," said Kyle.

"But it's time for a change," I reminded him.

"We're having a meeting here tomorrow night to talk about fixing it up," Mom told Dad as they went into the keeping room.

Ethan helped himself to a couple of hot dogs.

"Not so fast." Allison grabbed him. "Mom says they're to be used for the campaign."

"We're part of the campaign, aren't we? You have to feed the campaign."

I wanted to tell Mom about that debate with Tony Spano and maybe find out what an issue was. When I walked into the keeping room, she was saying something to Dad about Sam Jessup making her use that ridiculous speech about a football.

"I had my own speech all ready," Mom said. "He took it, handed me this paper, and said, 'Speak.'"

Dad saw me standing near the doorway. "What did you think about Mom's speech, B.J.?"

"It was okay, I guess."

But it wasn't. And Mom knew it wasn't.

"From now on, I'll write and give my own speeches," she said. "That is, as soon as I have an issue to write and talk about."

"Don't worry." Dad hugged her. "I think I found one for you. I was at the county court library today and came across an article in one of their papers. General Power and Gas wants to build power lines through Cranberry Falls."

"No! Power lines, Jack? You mean we'll have those huge steel towers going through our lovely town?"

"They want to build them right over our heads. How about that for an issue?"

I was sure relieved to hear we had an issue, even if it had to be something terrible like power lines over our heads. I didn't know much about them, except that it was how people got their electricity. And I'd seen the towers over in Middleview. You couldn't miss those monstrosities!

"I'll tell Sam Jessup and the others about it when they come over for the meeting tomorrow night," Mom said.

I followed them up the stairs.

"Better not say anything until we're certain it's happening," Dad told her as they went down the hallway.

"You're right, Jack. And if it *is* true, I'll wait and tell Cyrilla Cornsby when we open headquarters next week. It will be a perfect news release."

And then I'll have something to talk about in social studies, I thought, and went into my bedroom. I was too tired to remember if I told Mom about the debate. She must have been tired, too. Because she forgot to come in and say good night, like she always does.

★ ★ 3 ★ ★

Mom's Guardian Angel

FIRST THING Saturday morning, Nancy stopped by to pick up her mother's leftover mustard. I told her what a disaster the kickoff party had been.

"And they're all coming back for a meeting tonight!"

Nancy said she was glad it wasn't her mother they threw into the pool.

"What pool?"

"The political pool. My father says people plunge right in without realizing the consequences. Politics is a rough game."

MY MOTHER THE MAYOR, MAYBE

Nancy forgot the mustard. And it's a good thing. Mom was gone all day, and Allison had to borrow a few hot dogs from the freezer for lunch. We had them for dinner too, because when Mom got home, she had to get ready for the meeting.

The boys decided to camp out. Dad went to his office to get out of the way and catch up on some law work.

While Mom got dressed, Allison and I made some brownies. Actually, I made the brownies. Allison scraped the bowl and left me to clean up the mess because she was sleeping overnight at Amy Walker's.

I got stuck baby-sitting for Willie, upstairs. Mom was afraid he'd bark his head off at everybody.

I put on my favorite pajamas, an old pair of striped tiger ones that Ethan had grown out of. The elastic on the pants was loose and the stripes were faded, but they were the most comfortable pajamas in the world. I hopped into bed. Willie jumped in after me, growling at the noise below.

I could tell there were lots of people because cars kept coming in the driveway and the back door kept opening and closing beneath my room. And I could hear them laughing and talking, even though they were in the keeping room, because the noise comes right up through the cracks between the old floor—

boards. The smoke from that Mr. Jessup's cigar came right up, too. *Phew!* I got up to open a window. That's when I smelled those brownies.

I peeked out my door and down the back stairway. The coast was clear.

"I'm sure Mom won't mind if I get a couple of brownies, Willie. You stay in bed," I told him. "I'll bring you back a treat."

I tiptoed down, trying to skip the stairs that creaked. The kitchen was empty. I loaded a few brownies on a saucer and started back up to my room. Then I remembered Willie. I took a wooden bowl Mom had left out for pretzels to use for Willie's treat and opened the door to the broom closet under the stairs. That's where we keep Willie's dry dog food, in a big pail. I was lifting off the cover when I heard someone coming. I certainly didn't want to be caught in those crazy pajamas, so I closed the door a little and waited.

It was Mom. I could see her staring at the plate of brownies. She was wondering why it was a little empty. I started to push open the door and explain when Mr. Jessup came into the kitchen. I ducked back.

"Your speech went fine last night, Dorothy."

"Thank you, Sam. But from now on I think I'll write my own speeches."

MY MOTHER THE MAYOR, MAYBE

Through the crack I could see Mr. Jessup twitching his cigar from one side of his mouth to the other. He was also dropping ashes all over the kitchen floor and practically asphyxiating me.

Mom was pouring coffee in some cups on a tray. "I've been thinking, Sam. What the Democrats need is publicity. It might be a good idea to hire a P.R. man, you know, a public relations person to handle the publicity for us."

Mr. Jessup didn't think it was a good idea at all. I could tell by the funny look on his face.

He pretended to laugh. "That's preposterous, Dorothy! The Democrats don't have money to hire a P.R. man. Let's talk about something really important, like fixing up campaign headquarters next Saturday."

I watched him take the tray and walk with Mom toward the keeping room.

I filled the wooden bowl with Willie's surprise as fast as I could and headed back up the stairs. Halfway up, I felt something slipping. Darn it. It was that loose elastic. I put down Willie's treat and my saucer with the brownies so I could pull up my pajama bottoms. Wouldn't you know? At that very second, I heard Mr. Jessup talking. He was coming back into the kitchen! I held on to my pajama bottoms and ran.

When I reached the top of the stairs, I realized I'd left Willie's and my snack on the steps below. It was too late to run back down and get them, so I leaned against the stair wall and held my breath as I waited.

Mr. Jessup stood right at the bottom of the stairs, directly beneath me, with a skinny man I'd never seen before.

"What's the matter with you, Jessup?" the skinny man whispered. "You're letting that Pinkerton woman take over the whole campaign. Can't you stop her from talking so much about publicity? I don't like it."

"I don't like it either, Charlie."

So that was the skinny man's name. Charlie!

Mr. Jessup wiped his forehead with his handker-chief. When he put it back in his coat pocket where he keeps his cigars, I thought for sure he was going to light up another one. It was worse than that. He took one of my brownies off the saucer I'd left on the stairway and began eating it!

"I thought you said she was inexperienced," Charlie whoever-he-was said.

"She is." Mr. Jessup was talking with his mouth full of my brownie. "She doesn't know a thing about politics."

I leaned over a bit to try to get a better look at that

skinny guy and nearly fell down the stairs at what I saw.

Charlie was nibbling on Willie's dry dog food!

And Mr. Jessup took another one of my brownies!

"Stop worrying, Charlie. You know she hasn't got a chance. She's a sure loser." He stuffed the brownie in his mouth.

What did he mean by saying Mom was a "sure loser"? I wished he'd choke. But he didn't. He kept talking and eating my brownie.

"Just be glad she agreed to run, Charlie. She was the only one we could get. Don't worry. I'll keep her quiet."

"You'd better."

I couldn't believe what I was hearing. I couldn't believe what I was seeing, either. Charlie took another handful of Willie's surprise.

"Say, these are good." He picked up the wooden bowl. "Nice and crunchy and not too salty. I'm going to ask Dorothy what they are."

I gulped. But I didn't move. I waited for Mr. Jessup to follow Charlie back into the keeping room. He did. And he took the last brownie with him.

I was shaking, I was so mad. Not so much about the brownies, but because of what they said about Mom being a sure loser.

I walked slowly toward my bedroom, trying to figure out why they were talking like that behind Mom's back.

"Oh, there you are, Sam." It was Mom.

I sneaked over to the top of the stairs and listened.

"Everyone here tonight agrees with me. We've got to get a good P.R. man. It would do wonders for the Democrats. We might even have a chance to win."

"Watch those big ideas, Dorothy," Jessup said. "We have to work together—like a team—on this campaign. I told you, the Democrats haven't got the money for a public relations person."

"But we haven't even got our campaign literature."

"Give them time, Mrs. Pinkerton." It was that Charlie character talking.

"Time?" Mom was getting upset. "The campaign's already late getting started. You know that, Charlie."

"Well, the literature *does* have to be changed. It still has my name and picture on it."

I almost fell over the bannister. That's who the stranger was—Charlie Knots, the original Democratic candidate for mayor! The one Mom replaced because he was supposed to be so sick. If he thinks he's sick now, wait until he finds out he's eaten Willie's dog food, I thought as I crept back to my room.

I could hear Ethel Grove, the woman running for town clerk, reminding Mom she needed volunteers to clean out the railroad station. And then they were all saying good night.

"I almost forgot to ask you, Dorothy." It was Charlie Knots. "What were those delicious little things in the wooden bowl?"

I froze right in my tracks.

"Just pretzels, Charlie."

"Really? Well, I must say, they were mighty good."

I collapsed on my bed.

Willie growled.

"Don't blame me," I said and crawled under the covers. "I wasn't the one who ate your old treat. It was Charlie Knots."

The back door closed. Headlights began flashing in through my bedroom window. For a moment it was very still. A car drove in the driveway. It was Dad. It was so quiet without all those Democrats, I could hear every word Dad said when he opened the door.

"You've got your issue, Dorothy. It's a fact. General Power and Gas plans to put those towers right through Cranberry Falls. I read about it in the *Law Journal* at my office tonight."

"Wouldn't it be wonderful, Jack," Mom said, "if we could get some good publicity and try to stop them?"

"You will, Dorothy. Somewhere up there, you've got a guardian angel who's listening right now. And she's going to solve all those publicity problems for you."

I sat up. Dad was absolutely right! I wasn't exactly a guardian angel, but . . .

I hugged Willie. "Guess what?" I whispered. "I'm going to be Mom's P.R. angel."

★ ★ 4 ★ ★

An Angel for
a P.R. Person

I NEVER REALIZED what a long name Pinkerton is. I
was sewing the last *n* on Willie's sweater, and there
was barely room. I wanted to finish before Nancy
Tyler came over so I could show her. And then I'd tell
her the news. Not about the power lines. I remembered Mom said it would be best to wait and tell
Cyrilla Cornsby that news.

I knotted the thread and cut it. Then I checked the
lettering. It was a little crooked. But the way Willie
ran around when he had to wear his sweater, you'd
never notice.

I couldn't stop thinking about those two charac-
ters, Jessup and Knots. I never did tell Mom what I'd
heard. She'd be too upset, or say it was all my
imagination. Nancy was right. Politics is a rough
game. And I guess the real reason I didn't tell my
mother what those two said was because I was afraid
it was true—about her being a sure loser, I mean.
And the more I thought about it, the angrier I got.

As soon as Nancy pedaled up the driveway, I ran
outside and sat her down on the back porch steps.

"You'll never guess, so I'll tell you. I'm going to be
Mom's P.R. man."

"You mean P.R.P.—Public Relations Person,"
she corrected me.

"Oh. You know what it is." Sometimes that Nancy
can be too smart. "How come?"

"Everybody knows public relations means publicity. Besides, I've got an uncle in Yonkers who works
with P.R. people. He prints stuff for everybody, even
politicians. He's always giving me leftover balloons
and things."

"Oh. Well, how's this?" I held up Willie's red
knitted sweater. The white letters stood right out.
"See? 'Vote for Pinkerton.' "

"It's kind of small. Nobody could read it from a
distance. Too bad you can't put it on something

bigger." Nancy looked over toward the lower field where Allison was exercising Love. "Does your sister's horse have a sweater?"

"Of course not. Besides, she won't let anyone get near that horse. You know that. She even charges Marianne Spano for the privilege of mucking out the stall."

We both sat and watched Allison riding. And then I got another idea.

"Maybe your uncle would help me, Nancy."

"Huh?"

"Your uncle in Yonkers with all the balloons— could he help me with some publicity for Mom?"

"Well, I could ask him. Have you got a picture of her he could use to print on posters and things?"

I thought a moment. "Mr. Jessup is taking all the candidates to the photographer's today to have pictures taken for their new literature. I'll bet I could get one of those."

"That might take too long. It has to be developed and everything. You need one right now. There's not that much time before the election."

Nancy was right. "I know! There are some pictures in the attic. Come on!"

We dashed upstairs. I opened the attic door and flicked on the light switch. "There's lots of old

pictures in the cardboard boxes. You start looking.
I'll be right back."

Mom was in her bedroom getting ready. "How do
I look, B.J.?"

"Fine." I watched her brushing her hair. Allison
was right. She looked perfect, even if her hair was
short.

I thought I'd better ask her. "Is it okay for me to
be your P.R.P.—Public Relations Person?"

"Why, B.J." Mom smiled. "Of course." She put
down her brush and kissed me. "You're an angel."

"Huh?"

"And you can be my decorator, too. The railroad
station needs fixing for the opening. I promised Ethel
Grove we'd all help."

"Can Nancy come to the opening? She's going to
help me with your publicity."

"Everyone can come." Mom checked her make-up
in the mirror. "If I'm late, you'd better defrost some
hot dogs."

"Okay."

She hurried down the stairs.

"Don't forget to smile and take a good picture for
your P.R.P.," I yelled down at her.

Mom laughed. "You'll have it Saturday for the
opening," she called back.

I ran up to the attic.

Nancy was sitting on the floor in the middle of a pile of old photographs. "Here's a great one of your mother." She tossed it at me.

"That's when she was in high school. It's the senior class picnic. Don't you love her hair long like that?"

"Yeah, and she sure looks skinny in that two-piece bathing suit."

"It's my father's favorite picture."

"Then we'll use it."

"What are you talking about? We can't use this. It's too old. Besides, she's in that bathing suit. What would people say?"

Nancy took the picture and looked at it again. "Her face looks the same. And you said you liked her hair, didn't you? Uncle Al could cut off the bottom part and just use the face."

"He could do that?"

"Sure."

"Well, it's still too old." I put the picture back in the pile.

"But you can certainly recognize her," Nancy said.

I started down the stairs. "I don't think we should use it unless it's an emergency."

Nancy followed behind me. "What's the matter? Didn't you tell your mother you were going to be her P.R. person?"

"Of course I did. But we don't need to use that picture. Mom said the ones they're taking today will be at headquarters Saturday. That's soon enough. We'll give your Uncle Al one of those pictures to use."

"Okay." Nancy hopped on her bicycle. "Meanwhile, I'll ask him what he can do for us." She coasted out the driveway.

I went down to the cellar and dug out some old paint. I wanted to make a few signs to put on telephone poles around town. I knew the telephone company didn't like signs on their poles, but I figured if it increased their business, they wouldn't mind. I decided, **Call on Dorothy Pinkerton— She's a good operator,** would help us both.

"Trouble was, it took me an hour to finish one sign. I was getting started on another when the phone rang.

It was Nancy. "Beej." (She always calls me that when she's excited.) "Beej, you'll never guess what. My Uncle Al came up from Yonkers for dinner. He says he'll be happy to print something for your mother. He says he's a Democrat, too, and it won't cost you much at all. Mom thought he was a Republican—but that was last year."

"That's fantastic, Nancy. Did he have any suggestions?"

"Well, he's got a lot of blotters in stock. He said since the ball-point pen was invented, blotters aren't so popular. You can have thousands for practically nothing."

"Really?"

"Uh-huh. What do you want to say on it?"

I knew right away! "Blot out the Republicans with Dorothy Pinkerton for mayor."

"Hey, you really are a P.R.P. That sounds great. I'll tell him. And he might be able to get you some pencils and buttons or pins. He's got lots of stuff left over. People use everything for publicity. One year the deliveryman for a diaper service was running for some big office. He had Uncle Al print 'Time for a change' on dozens of diapers and gave them to all his customers. There might be some disposable ones left over."

"I don't think we should use the diapers, Nancy, but the pins and pencils sound good."

"Okay. Get busy and think of some things for Uncle Al to print on them." Nancy hung up.

I felt wonderful. I was a good P.R. person, like Nancy said. And with some good publicity, I could get the whole town to vote for Mom.

I ran back down to the cellar and began painting some more telephone pole signs. Uncle Al could probably print hundreds of signs for me in no time at all. And Nancy said he had lots of publicity stuff left over besides the pencils and pins.

I put down my paintbrush.

Let's see, if I got the pencils I'd print on them—uh—**Get to the point. Sharpen up with Dorothy Pinkerton.** No. That would be better on the pins. And if they were big enough, maybe Uncle Al could add, **Don't get stuck with Mayor Quinn.**

I wondered if he had any leftover erasers. That would be easy. **Erase Mayor Quinn.**

I sat down on the cellar floor. The greatest would be if I could think of some publicity for that power-line issue. But what could I say? And what would I put it on?

Let's see. **Issue . . . miss you?**—no. Uh, **issue . . . tissue!** How about, **Don't forget the issue written on this tissue!**

No, that doesn't say anything. I closed my eyes so I could think real hard.

I got it! **Don't sneeze at the power-line issue.** Sneeze—that's good. . . . Uh, **When you use this tissue, wipe up Mayor Quinn.** No—but maybe . . . **Wipe out Mayor Quinn. Vote Dorothy Pinkerton in!** That's it!

I jumped up and stepped right on the wet

paintbrush. I now had one yellow shoe. I didn't care. I had to call Nancy right away.

I took the cellar steps two at a time.

"Nancy, is your Uncle Al still there?"

"Uh-huh. Why?"

"I just thought of the greatest P.R. idea for Mom and the Democrats. Ask your Uncle Al if he's ever printed anything on tissue."

"Tissue? Hey, that's a stupendous idea."

"Isn't it? I knew you'd love it."

"I'm sure he probably has. He's printed slogans on everything else. Hold on. I'll ask him if he has any rolls left over."

"Rolls? Nancy, wait a minute. Not toilet paper rolls! I mean tissue like you blow your nose on."

"Oh. Okay." Nancy sounded disappointed. "And that's a pretty good idea, too, B.J. You sure are a great P.R. person."

★ ★ 5 ★ ★

Off and Running

CRANBERRY FALLS doesn't have any cranberries. It doesn't have any falls either—just a little brook that runs along the cornfields behind Town Hall and the railroad station. It was named after one of the early settlers, Joshua Cranberry.

Allison says she read in a book that he couldn't learn to ride his horse and was always falling off, so that's how the town got its name, Cranberry Falls. I don't believe it.

One good thing, though. It's not that big. The center of the town is all squashed together. And from the railroad station you can see the whole business section from beginning to end.

I was helping Ethel Grove's husband staple red, white, and blue bunting on the station house. Kyle was building a little platform in front of us between the overgrown tracks and the sidewalk. It was for the Mudheads. When Kyle told them there'd be free food, they volunteered to play at the opening.

Ethan and Jon were up on the roof winding strings of Christmas lights around some drainpipes.

When I finished helping Mr. Grove with the material, I had to stand on an old wooden box and hold the **All aboard with the Democrats** sign so he could nail it over the door. I tried not to look across the street at the Republican headquarters. Mr. Spano had rented a storefront, and big pictures of Mayor Quinn were plastered all over the windows. That jerk Tony Spano was standing in the doorway passing out campaign buttons. He was wearing a stupid straw hat with a band on it that said, **Win with Quinn.**

I wondered where Mr. Jessup was with Mom's pictures and if Nancy would arrive in time to help me pass out the new literature.

As I stepped off the box, I noticed a telephone pole I'd missed way down the street. It was covered with bushes, but if I could somehow reach above them, it would be a perfect spot for another **Call on Dorothy Pinkerton—She's a good operator** sign.

I headed down the sidewalk with the box and hammer and nails.

A man was standing near the bushes next to the pole. What luck! It was Mr. Jessup. I could tell him about being Mom's P.R. person and ask him for a few pictures to put up with my sign.

As I got closer, I realized it wasn't only the bushes he was standing next to. Mayor Quinn was there. That's pretty strange, I thought, those two being together like that.

Another man was with them who looked skinny enough to be Charlie Knots, but I couldn't tell for sure. He handed Mr. Jessup a package and disappeared behind the bushes.

Sam Jessup has a bad memory. He didn't recognize me until I told him I was going to be Mom's P.R. woman.

"Really? Well," he said, twitching his cigar, "that's very good."

He's rude, too. He never introduced me to Mayor Quinn. And before I could ask about Mom's pictures, they walked away.

When I stood on the box, I couldn't reach high

enough to put up my sign. But I could still see Mayor Quinn and Mr. Jessup talking down the street. It looked suspicious, if you ask me.

I got back to the station as Mom and Dad arrived. Allison jumped out of the back of the car with the hot dogs and Willie. Willie was all dressed up in his campaign sweater.

"You'd better tie him someplace," I told Allison. "When Kyle and the Mudheads start that music, Willie will go crazy with the noise."

But Willie ran over to the table where Jon was giving Ethel Grove an extension cord for her big coffee maker. Allison followed him with the hot dogs.

Kyle and the Mudheads were on the platform setting up their music stands. In a matter of seconds you could hear them all over town—Kyle beating on the drums, the trumpeter blowing his trumpet, and the fellow with the guitar playing a harmonica at the same time.

Across the street, I could see Tony Spano holding his nose. I didn't care. People were coming from every direction over to the railroad station, and Mom was laughing and shaking hands and talking to everybody.

I spotted Mr. Jessup hurrying down the sidewalk carrying the package.

Allison came running toward me. "Where's Willie?"

"Huh?" I could barely hear her, the music was so loud.

"That newspaper reporter Cyrilla Cornsby's here," she yelled. "She'll want to take a picture of Willie in his sweater."

"He's probably hiding somewhere from the noise," I yelled back. "I told you to tie him up. Have you seen Nancy Tyler?"

Allison shook her head and strolled over to the platform, pretending to look for Willie. Cyrilla was setting up her camera, and Allison wanted to be sure to get in the picture.

I walked over to the table where Ethel Grove was serving the refreshments. Mr. Jessup had left his package there, next to the coffee maker.

"Would you like to pass out some of these?" Mrs. Grove shouted. "It's our new publicity." She handed me a small pamphlet. "Mr. Jessup picked them up at the printers. I always take a bad picture."

Ethel Grove was right.

But then I saw the rest of the candidates. Joe Belluci looked like a gangster. Tom Crawford was cross-eyed, and Mom, my beautiful Mom, looked like a witch. It was sabotage, like someone had made everyone look bad on purpose!

Mom was standing in the doorway of the station with Mr. Jessup. I grabbed a couple of hot dogs and headed toward them. I'd give them each one. And then, as their P.R. person, I'd also give them my opinion of those pictures. "To tell you the truth, Mr. Jessup," I'd say, "you need a new photographer."

By the time I got through the crowd, Mom and Mr. Jessup had disappeared inside the station house. When I poked my head in, they were having an argument. Mr. Jessup was shaking his cigar right in Mom's face and saying he didn't want her to tell the newspaper about the power lines.

I decided I'd better give the hot dogs to the Mudheads.

As I walked over toward the platform, Cyrilla was about to take their picture. Allison was standing as close to the platform as she could without being hit on the head with one of Kyle's drumsticks.

Suddenly, Willie appeared. He must have been hiding under the platform. I guess he couldn't stand the noise anymore. He began turning around in circles and getting all mixed up in the extension wires Jon had used to connect everything. Before I could rescue him, he was so tangled up in the cords he couldn't get out.

And he must have yanked out all the plugs. The

music got real soft. The microphone toppled over, and the Mudheads stopped playing. What a relief! All you could hear was some woman shouting at the top of her lungs.

I turned to see what was going on. It was Mom! She was in the doorway of the station, yelling at Mr Jessup. And she was so angry she didn't realize the music had stopped.

"I don't care what you say," she shouted at him. "I'm going to tell Cyrilla Cornsby about the power lines going through Cranberry Falls."

Cyrilla left her camera in the middle of the sidewalk and was flying over to Mom.

Everyone, including Willie and me, followed her.

"What's this about the power lines?" she asked.

Mr. Jessup was so anxious not to have Mom speak, he didn't even take the cigar out of his mouth. "Power lines?" he repeated. "Oh, yes. That's right. This campaign's got *power* and our *lines* are right up front like a battlefield. But we have to wait until the enemy appears before we use our ammunition." He looked at Mom. "You understand, Dorothy?"

"Yes, Sam. But I don't think you do. The enemy *has* appeared."

"Enemy?" Cyrilla began writing like crazy. "What enemy?"

"The marching monsters," Mom told her.

"Marching monsters?" Cyrilla looked around. "Where are the marching monsters?"

"In Middleview," said Mom, "and they're headed this way."

"What?"

"They're also called overhead high-tension wires, Cyrilla." And then Mom said it, right out. "General Power and Gas has applied for a permit to put power lines straight through our town and right over our heads. And I think the voters should know about it."

Mr. Jessup nearly swallowed his cigar. When he stopped choking, he said, "I've got some important new material on the candidates for the newspaper, Cyrilla." He headed for the table.

And that's when I saw the mess. When Willie got caught in the extension wires, one of them must have been connected to the coffee maker. It was tipped over, and all the new publicity was buried in coffee grounds.

"It's ruined!" Mr. Jessup screamed at poor Mrs. Grove.

I could see Nancy crossing the street carrying a huge grocery bag.

"It's an emergency," I said as I ran over to meet her. "Willie spilled coffee all over the new literature.

But never mind, the pictures were awful anyway."

Nancy smiled and handed me the bag. "Surprise!" she said. "I'm late because I put one in every mailbox I passed on the way over. And I gave one to everyone I bumped into on the street. They love them."

"Love what?"

"Your blotters—from Uncle Al!"

"He printed them already?" I reached into the bag and pulled out a couple.

I nearly fainted.

"You—you used the picture," I finally gasped.

"Isn't it great?"

"You sneaked Mom's picture out of the attic and I said to.wait." I was in a state of shock. "How could you do a thing like that?"

"Well, B.J., you said you'd use it in an emergency. And didn't you just tell me when I arrived that it's an emergency?"

"Yes, but you didn't know that when you gave your uncle the picture." I took another look and groaned. "Besides, I thought we agreed to have only Mom's head. You said he'd cut off the bottom part and just use the face. He printed half the picture."

"What are you talking about? You wanted all her hair, didn't you? He couldn't cut that off. It wouldn't look right."

"But Nancy, she looks like she's in her under-wear."

"Underwear?"

"You know, her brassiere."

"Oh. Well, just explain it's the top of her bathing suit."

"Nancy, there are hundreds of blotters. Oh, my gosh! What will my father say?"

"Your father loves the picture, remember? And your mother needs the publicity. Listen." Nancy took my arm. "This is the opening of your campaign headquarters! And it's really the beginning of the race. You know, like a horse race when the starter yells, 'They're off and running!' "

"You're the one who's off," I told her. I could see Mr. Jessup walking over toward us! "But I think we'd better both start running."

I picked up the bag. "You've got to get back every blotter you passed out," I whispered, "or I'll never speak to you again."

All of a sudden Nancy looked worried. She knew I meant business. "I will. I'll swear on the Bible," said Nancy. "I'll get every one back."

Mr. Jessup was looking at us kind of funny. I pulled Nancy over near the platform and shoved the bag at her. "Hide these in the Mudheads' guitar case while I go help Ethel Grove clean up the coffee grounds."

"Sure. But don't be so nervous, B.J. Relax. I'll get back all the blotters and have Uncle Al put a blouse on each one of them."

"You'd better," I warned her. "Immediately!"

★ ★ 6 ★ ★
Marching Monsters vs. Allison's Horse

It was the best headquarters opening the Democrats ever had. Because even though Willie ruined Mr. Jessup's literature and I couldn't pass out my blotters, the publicity was wonderful. Cyrilla managed to get the power-line issue all over the front page of the *Courier*. The headlines are right here in my scrapbook: **Democrats Say High-Tension Power Lines, Like Marching Monsters, May Be Heading Toward Cranberry Falls.**

Sunday afternoon, Dad drove us all over to Middleview. That's where General Power and Gas

had already put their power lines. I'd noticed them
before, but I guess if they're not in your own backyard, you don't think about them. Mom says that's
the way it is. Unless something affects you personally, you really don't care. So that's at least one good
thing about getting involved in politics. You start
caring about more than just yourself.

We jumped out of the car and walked over toward
the hillside to get a better look at the steel towers.
You'd think a giant steamroller had gone right over
the top of the hill and smashed everything under it.
All the trees and flowers were gone. Instead, there
were these giant towers sticking way up in the sky
with ugly, heavy wires connecting them. They were
monsters, like Mom said. And the scary thing was,
they really did look like they were marching, right
over the hills to Cranberry Falls.

"These ugly things may go through our town?"
moaned Allison. "It's absolutely gross."

For once I agreed with her. "Gross" was sure the
right word.

"What'll happen to the wild animals when they
cut down all the trees?" worried Ethan.

"They'll be displaced," said Mom, "just like they
probably were here. And so will a lot of people. If
those high-tension wires go through Cranberry Falls,

we'll lose homes and part of the state park."

"The state park?" asked Kyle. "Hey, that's right next to our lower field."

"The lower field where I keep Love?" said Allison. Mom and Dad nodded.

"Oh, no," she cried. "What will happen to my horse if they put those things through our field?"

"It's not only a question of what will happen to your horse, Allison," Mom said.

"There will be a lot of questions about what might happen to the people nearby," said Dad.

"Then why are they thinking of doing such a gross thing?" Allison wanted to know.

"People need electricity, stupid," said Jon. "There's a power plant up north where they make electricity. The towers and wires are how they send it to the cities."

"There's two sides to everything, you know, Allison," said Kyle.

"That's true," said Mom.

"But there must be a way to get electricity to the people without ruining everything," I said.

"There is," said Mom. "Power lines can go underground, if they're really necessary. The problem is the consumer may have to pay more, but in the long run it'll be worth it."

We stood there, looking.

Then Dad said what we were all thinking. "The sad fact is, these giant erector sets could soon be sitting in our backyard."

We're always having family conferences when there's trouble. So when Dad called one that night, I nearly died. I thought for sure someone had seen those blotters. But Dad began by saying we should try to help Mom win the election so that she could stop the power lines. That was the first time Dad said anything serious about Mom's winning, and the whole family got excited. Allison volunteered to write to the President for help. When the boys laughed, she said she was only kidding. But I know Allison. From the minute she thought Mom might be mayor, she had visions of moving into the White House, horse and all.

The boys promised to go doorbell ringing. I told them I could get them something to pass out real soon, like blotters, maybe.

"Blotters?" asked Allison. "What for?"

"Publicity," I told them. "I'm Mom's public relations person."

"What?" Dad was surprised.

"Mom and Mr. Jessup said it was all right. And

Nancy Tyler's uncle in Yonkers can print things for us."

"Wait a minute, B.J.," said Dad. "You'd better leave the literature to Mr. Jessup."

"Goodness, yes," agreed Mom. "He's in charge of that. He won't like it if you do publicity only for me, B.J. He wants all the candidates to work together, like a team."

"By the looks of his literature, I'm not sure which team he's on," I said. "I saw him talking to Mayor Quinn Saturday and Charlie Knots was there. And they looked pretty friendly, if you ask me."

Dad laughed. "Well, they should. They've been friends for years, B.J. Just because they belong to different political parties doesn't mean they can't be friends."

"And Sam Jessup is having more material printed." Mom put her arm around me. "You'll think of other ways to help."

"Well, I'm going to debate Tony Spano in social studies about the issues," I told her.

"Now that's being a P.R. person!" said Dad. "Your whole class will know about the power lines, and they'll tell their parents, and that gets votes for Mom."

"And I'll give you the information so you'll know what you're talking about," added Mom.

Dad ended the conference with a warning. "Remember, when you get in politics, you're always in the public eye. So stay out of trouble. Everyone will be watching you. Most of all, keep cool, calm, and collected. And remember, every vote counts!"

I was standing in line at the cafeteria. Nancy ran up and stood behind me.

"Guess what?" she whispered. "Everyone's talking about your mother."

"Oh, no! They found out about the blotters?"

"Don't be silly. I mean, they're talking about those awful power lines. Even my parents might vote for your mother. And they've never voted for a Democrat in their lives. And Uncle Al has some more free publicity for her."

I took my lunch money out of my sneaker and gave it to Mrs. Perry behind the counter. "Look, Nancy. Dad said that Mr. Jessup should take over the literature and that I have to be very careful from now on not to get into any trouble. So where are those blotters? Did you give them back to your Uncle Al to fix?" I picked up my pizza and went over to the table.

Nancy followed me. "B.J., listen. It's not literature. It's balloons."

"Balloons?"

"Yup. They were left over from a Boy Scout

convention. They have 'Be Prepared' printed on them."

I thought a moment. "Could he add something like—uh—'Be Prepared . . . for Dorothy Pinkerton to pull down the power lines'?"

"Of course! B.J. Pinkerton, you are a great P.R. person."

"Thanks, Nancy, but what about the blotters? Can Uncle Al fix them?"

"Well . . ."

I waited while Nancy took a bite of my pizza.

"Well . . . oh, my gosh." She nudged me. "I hate to spoil your appetite, but look over there."

It was Tony Spano. He still had on that old straw hat. A lot of kids were standing around him, and he was giving away bumper stickers. The kids were plastering them all over their books and the cafeteria tables and everything.

"I wish we could get some bumper stickers, Nancy."

"They're awfully expensive, B.J."

"I guess I'll have to use the balloons then." I took back my pizza. "When will your uncle have them ready?"

"In about a week," Nancy said.

When the bell rang, we walked together down the hallway to social studies watching that Tony Spano handing out his old bumper stickers and sticking them on the lockers and walls. It was disgusting.

As soon as we sat down, Mr. Shattelles began talking about the power lines. He said it would be a perfect issue for the debate.

Tony Spano raised his hand. "I've got a better issue. The Republicans uncovered an old law in our town that prohibits keeping a horse on your property unless you have at least five acres."

Mr. Shattelles looked puzzled. "Why would that be an issue, Tony?"

"The Pinkertons keep a horse on their property, and they only have four acres."

"And how would you know that?" It was my friend Nancy, yelling from the other side of the room.

"My father told me," he yelled back at her. "Besides, it's public knowledge. The acreage of every taxpayer is posted at Town Hall. And the zoning law is down there too."

I tried to sit still and remain cool, calm, and collected, like Dad said you should. I even sat on my hands so I wouldn't throw my social studies book at that idiot.

"Exactly what makes that an issue, Tony?" Mr. Shattelles asked.

"Mrs. Pinkerton is breaking a zoning law."

The next thing I knew, the whole class was in a big argument over who was breaking the law, Mom or the horse. I didn't have a chance to say one word about those awful steel towers. And when Mr. Shattelles got up to write our homework assignment on the blackboard, everyone giggled. He'd been sitting on a **Keep Quinn In** bumper sticker.

As soon as Nancy and I got on the bus, we told Allison about the old zoning law the Republicans had found. She got hysterical.

"I'm going to lose my horse," she wailed.

Mike Callahan had to threaten to throw her off the bus to quiet her down.

"I'll do anything to beat those Republicans," she whimpered. "I'm going campaigning as soon as I get home."

"Good," I said. "I'll go with you. But there's nothing to hand out."

"I'll think of something," she muttered.

Nancy said we should buy a dozen diapers.

"Sure! Like Uncle Al's diaper man. He printed 'Time for a change' on all these diapers, Allison," I said.

Allison interrupted me. "That's gross! But it *is* time for a change."

So when we got home, we made a huge picture of a

clock. Under it we printed, **Time for a change. Vote for Dorothy Pinkerton.** I added, **and all her team** in real small print.

I guess you could say it was Allison's horse and the marching monsters that pushed the whole family into the political pool. Or maybe we just jumped in. Anyway, from then on you could feel things changing. People stopped us on the street. They all said how awful Mayor Quinn was not to tell the voters about those power lines.

Things began changing at home, too. Mom was out more than ever. The telephone was ringing all the time. Poor Willie! He was so dizzy from turning around in circles, he could hardly walk. The only thing that didn't change was the menu. It was always the same—hot dogs.

⋆ ⋆ 7 ⋆ ⋆

Willie Is Kidnapped!

NANCY AND I were sitting on the back steps waiting. A deliveryman drove into the driveway.

"It's the balloons," I shouted, and ran to get the package.

"Don't be too sure," said Nancy. "You'd better throw some water on it."

"What are you talking about?"

"It might be a bomb. Don't you remember that scary television show? When the good guy found out about the crooks—"

"I remember." I began opening the package. "The bad guys tried to stop him from telling the newspapers. Just like when Mr. Jessup tried to stop Mom from telling Cyrilla about the power lines."

"He did? That's a weird coincidence. What happened?"

"Not a thing. And Cyrilla put it in the paper, didn't she?" I pulled out a handful of balloons.

"Aren't they beautiful?" Nancy grabbed one and started blowing it up.

I watched Mom's name get bigger and bigger. "Maybe we should have put the other candidates' names on it too, Nancy."

"Huh?"

"You know—'like a team,' Mom said."

"Believe me, B.J., there's no room. Besides, the balloons are a gift for your mother from my uncle on account of the mistake he made on the blotters. Where's all the literature Mr. Jessup was taking care of? Let the team use that."

"Okay." I put the balloons back in the box. "But I think I'll keep them in my room until we decide how to use them. Maybe by then your Uncle Al will have fixed the blotters and we can pass them out together. How about that?"

Nancy suddenly realized she had to get home for dinner.

I sat on the steps for a while, just thinking. That Nancy. She always gets excited and starts exaggerating everything, like that bomb on a silly TV show. But the more I thought about that show, the more it reminded me of Sam Jessup trying to keep Mom from telling the newspaper about those power lines. And where was all that literature he promised Mom? I didn't trust that man. And I still hadn't forgiven him for saying Mom was a sure loser. Whose side was he on, anyway? If he was a Democrat and Mom's campaign manager, he shouldn't hang around with that Republican, Mayor Quinn—even if they are best friends. And where did that other character, Charlie Knots, fit in? I bet he was the one responsible for those awful pictures! Things were so mixed up, I couldn't tell the good guys from the bad guys.

I looked at the balloons again. What was it Mom said? "Mr. Jessup won't like it if you do publicity only for me, B.J."

I wished I'd at least had Joe Belluci's name printed on them, too. I shivered and closed the box.

I was sure Nancy was right. Something was wrong. It was more than a weird coincidence! The next time a package arrived in the mail, I'd throw a bucket of water on it.

Allison and I were in the kitchen. The boys had already left for the high school, and we had half an hour before our bus came. We were squirting **Vote for Pinkerton** on large dog biscuits with Mom's cake decorator. There were an awful lot of dogs running loose around Cranberry Falls, and we needed the biscuits so we could go campaigning for Mom after school.

The phone rang.

"You answer, B.J." Dad grabbed his coat and left for his office.

Willie ran out the door, too. That telephone was driving the whole family crazy.

It was some woman asking if Mom was for fluoridation.

"What's fluoridation?" I yelled upstairs to Mom.

"The town puts fluoride in the water to help your teeth—and yes, I'm for it."

"She's for it," I told the woman.

"Well, she just lost my vote." The woman slammed the receiver in my ear.

Mom came down the back stairs. "Mayor Quinn's for it, too. The town's going to get fluoridation no matter who gets elected. Who was it?"

"It sounded like that old Mrs. Hally."

"If it was, I don't know why she's so worried," Allison said. "She doesn't even have any teeth."

Willie was barking outside at the garbage truck

in the driveway. I ran out to talk to the garbage collectors because, like Dad says, every vote counts.

While the men emptied the garbage cans, I followed them and explained about the overhead high-tension wires.

"It's not that my mother's against electricity, but it's all the damage the overhead wires will do. Mom says if they could put them underground, like our garbage pails, it would be okay."

"What do you mean?" the driver asked as the men carried the empty cans back behind the porch.

"Remember when the garbage pails were above the ground, how ugly and smelly they were? You told Dad to dig a hole and put those steel cylinders in the ground to hold the pails."

"Oh, yeah! And he was worried the lids would be too heavy to lift. I told him they were made just heavy enough so that the raccoons couldn't get in the garbage."

"And see how beautifully they're buried there?" I pointed to where the men were putting the cans back in the ground. "Even the flies can't find the garbage pails!"

We all shook hands. The men hopped back on the truck.

"Don't forget to vote for Mom," I yelled as they left. "And remember why."

WILLIE IS KIDNAPPED!

"Sure," the driver yelled back. "She's for underground garbage pails."

"It's underground power lines," I shouted.

I could hear the telephone ringing.

Mom dashed out the door. She was on her way to another Meet the Candidates coffee.

The school bus was stopping out front. I waved for Mike, the driver, to wait. I could see Allison inside, talking. It looked important.

"Who was it?" I asked as we both ran for the bus.

"A man taking some poll."

"To see if Mom's going to beat Mayor Quinn?"

"No. To find out what television shows I watched last night."

We always took Willie with us when we went campaigning. But that afternoon when Allison and I got off the bus, Willie was missing. The boys said he wasn't waiting at the gate when they got home, and he wasn't inside either.

We couldn't believe it. In all the years we've had Willie, he's hardly ever gone off the property.

"The Republicans probably kidnapped him," said Allison. "It's one of those dirty tricks you always read about in politics."

"You're crazy," Jon told her. "Why would the Republicans kidnap Willie?"

MY MOTHER THE MAYOR, MAYBE

"To stop us from campaigning," she said. "It's part of their strategy. Everyone knows how much Willie means to Mom and this family."

"Get your dog biscuits and come on," said Kyle. "We can look for Willie while we're ringing door-bells. He's most likely in some neighborhood right now, campaigning by himself."

We decided if the boys took one side of the street and Allison and I got the houses on the other side, it would be faster. And, that way, we might find Willie sooner.

The first house we went to, the lady slammed the door in our faces the minute we mentioned Mom's name. When we read the name on the mailbox, we knew why. It was Mayor Quinn's wife.

The next house was full of screaming kids and barking dogs. A tired housewife opened the door. I *thought* it was a tired housewife. The man's hair was all messed up and his apron was covered with flour. He looked so worn out that I was afraid to tell him I smelled his cake burning. And the baby he was holding was crying its head off.

Allison handed the poor man a few dog biscuits. "They're great for teething," she told him.

"Vote for Dorothy Pinkerton!" I said.

"Dorothy?" he asked.

I nodded.

He slammed the door on us, too, but before it closed, I heard what he said: "A woman's place is in the home."

In between houses, we'd take turns running across the street to see if the boys had found Willie. They hadn't, and my feet were starting to hurt.

The third house was much better.

"Why, it's Dorothy Pinkerton's girls," the nice lady said.

"We want you to vote for our mother," Allison usually began.

And then I'd add, "And all her team."

We never had a chance.

"I went to school with your mother. You tell her she has my vote. I know Dorothy will do a bang-up job, once she gets elected."

I poked Allison. "We have to be going."

"Of course you do." The woman smiled at us. "You want to tell everybody to vote for your mom. Well, don't you worry. She's going to win. I'll guarantee it. I'll make certain everyone I know votes for her."

"Thanks, that's wonderful," I said as we hurried down the walk.

"Tell Dorothy I think she'll make a great president," the woman called.

We stopped.

"President?" I called back. "She's running for mayor."

"Mayor? I thought she was running for president of the P.T.A.!"

It was a relief when no one answered the next few doors. But Allison always said she saw someone peeking out the window. So she'd ring the doorbell again and again, while I rested my feet.

The boys weren't doing any better. I could see them across the street getting doors slammed in their faces, too. And then we heard Jon shouting. I thought they'd found Willie. Instead, Kyle was in a big fight with this kid. They were rolling all over someone's lawn. We ran to help.

Kyle already had the fellow pinned to the ground. "My mother's going to raise your father's taxes," he said.

"That doesn't sound like the right thing to say," I told him.

Ethan came running up the sidewalk. Three dogs were chasing him. I was hoping one might be Willie—no such luck.

"Help," he yelled as he went past us. "They're friendly, but they're hungry. I need more biscuits."

The biggest "friendly" dog was grabbing Ethan's pants. We had to rescue him and use all the dog biscuits to get rid of the dogs.

It was getting late. Everyone was tired and grouchy and worried about Willie. Especially when we got home, and he wasn't there.

Kyle promised that he and Dad would drive around later and look for him.

Allison started making supper.

"Can't we have something besides hot dogs?" asked Ethan.

"How can you think of food at all—especially hot dogs!" I said.

"I thought you were the one who loved them Ethan," Allison said.

"Not three times a day. Put some scrambled eggs or something over them."

"Or learn to cook a pot roast the way Mom does," said Jon.

I was setting the table when I heard howling and whimpering. It sounded muffled and way off somewhere.

"Hey, everybody," I shouted as I ran to the back door. "I think it's Willie!"

"Where?" Allison said.

"Outside."

Kyle opened the door, and Allison dashed out toward the front of the house. The boys headed down the driveway. I went behind the back porch.

I heard the sound again. It was somewhere real

close to the side of the house. It was coming from the underground garbage pails! I opened the lid and looked down. It was Willie! He was stuck in an underground garbage pail!

"I found him," I shouted.

They all came running.

"The garbage collector must have left the lid open this morning," I explained as the boys pulled him out. "And the lids close so easily, it must have closed by itself after Willie fell in."

"I'll bet he was looking for something to eat," mumbled Jon.

"Wait until Mom hears you were lost and found in the garbage, Willie!" I said.

But Mom didn't pay any attention when we told her at dinner. She was too busy reading the *Courier*.

"Listen to this, everybody. 'Dorothy Pinkerton's power-line issue has made the coming election the most important in years. For the first time His Honor, Mayor Quinn, has a formidable opponent.' "

"What's that mean?" I asked.

"It means Mom is going to win!" said Allison.

"Oh, Allison." Mom laughed. But she didn't say she didn't have a chance, like before.

After dinner, Mom had to meet with the other candidates.

WILLIE IS KIDNAPPED!

It was my turn to do the dishes. Willie trotted after me into the kitchen.

"Don't worry," I told him as I waited for him to lick the plates. "Things will be back to normal in a few weeks. You'll be eating pot roast instead of hot dogs. And Mom will be out here in the kitchen serving dessert, like she used to."

Willie stopped licking the plates and looked up at me.

"Well, either Mom or maybe a maid, if Mom gets elected," I said.

Willie growled.

"Aha! You're just mad because you're not getting enough attention." I picked up the plates. "Boy, are you spoiled. All your life Mom's been doing things for you. It's not going to hurt us to do something for her for a change, is it? Like make her mayor, maybe."

Later that evening, someone rang the doorbell and left a package on the front porch. I wasn't taking any chances. I ran to the kitchen to get a bucket of water.

By the time I got back, Allison had opened it.

I couldn't believe what I saw. It was the Democrats' campaign literature. Mr. Jessup hadn't changed a thing. It was that same old pamphlet with the horrible pictures!

I should have thrown the water on it, like Nancy said.

★ ★ 8 ★ ★

A P.R. Person's Dream Come True

I WAS IN THE keeping room drawing some maps of Cranberry Falls for the debate with Tony Spano. Mom and Dad were helping me. The lights were on out in the barn. Through the window I could see the freshman float committee. They'd been using the barn to work on their float for Homecoming Weekend. They were finally leaving.

As soon as they did, Ethan ran in. "Want to see the float that's going to win first prize tomorrow?" he shouted. "Come out to the barn everybody!"

It didn't look like any first prize to me. All they

did was cover an old wagon with paper flowers. There was a huge dome, covered with vegetables, sitting in the middle of the wagon. That was supposed to be the world. It had pieces of cabbage stuck on it for the oceans and broccoli and potatoes for the land.

"That's only half of it. Look!" Ethan pointed to a big cage filled with birds. "They're going to be hidden inside the globe! There's a trick opening. A big sign pops up. 'Peace on Earth,' it says. Then, all these homecoming pigeons fly out."

"You mean *homing* pigeons," Kyle said.

"I wish the sophomores had thought of that," said Jon. "All we have is a rocket that smokes."

"That's really neat, Ethan," said Kyle. "Where did you get the pigeons?"

"They belong to Gerard. He's the chairman of the float committee."

"What's the trick that opens the globe?" I wanted to know.

"Gerard."

"Gerard?" Mom and Dad asked.

"He's going to be inside."

"With all the pigeons?" I asked.

Ethan grinned. "We've got it all worked out."

Love whinnied from down below in the carriage

shed. Allison opened the trap door where the stairs go down to the stall.

"Are you hungry, my Love?" she hollered down the steps.

"That horse is always hungry," said Dad. "It costs more to feed that horse than the whole family."

"I'd better get her some carrots," Allison said and ran back to the house.

We followed her.

Ethan was so excited he walked backward all the way, laughing and bragging about how the freshman float would win first prize for sure.

"Too bad the Democrats couldn't have a float," I said. "It would be great publicity."

The next morning I got up early. I wanted to see how Gerard was going to fit inside that thing with all those pigeons. I also wanted to stick a few **Vote for Pinkerton** signs on the wagon wheels.

Dad was driving Mom to the radio station. She and Mayor Quinn were being interviewed about the power lines.

"It's being taped, B.J.," said Mom. "They'll broadcast it tomorrow, and you can take notes for your debate."

"Good luck, Mom."

"Thanks, B.J. Just pray that the mayor at least

makes up his mind. He's been so wishy-washy about the power-line issue, nobody knows how he feels about it yet." She hurried out.

"Tell Ethan we'll be back in time to see his float at the high school," Dad called from the car.

I ran out to the barn.

At first I thought I was seeing things. The wagon was empty except for a big round ball of chicken wire. And Love was eating what was left of the class float! Allison must have forgotten to close the trap door after she gave Love the carrots.

Something flew over my head. I looked up. Hundreds of pigeons were sitting on the beams. That horse must have pushed the cage door open with her nose.

Poor Ethan. What a catastrophe!

I tied Love to a pine tree and dashed into the house to tell everybody.

Ethan raced to the barn. We were all right behind him.

"It's ruined," he moaned, running around the float. "That horse ate everything—the vegetables, the flowers, the whole world!" He rushed over to the pigeon cage and collapsed on the barn floor. "Oh, no! She even ate Gerard's pigeons!"

"They're up there, Eeth," I said.

"Where?" he wailed.

I pointed to the rafters.

"They'll never come down," he cried.

"They're homing pigeons," said Kyle. "They'll go home eventually."

"But Gerard and the committee will be here any minute to pull the float over to the high school!"

"Can't you fix it?" said Allison.

He nearly hit her. "The whole freshman class has been working on it for two months, and you want me to fix it in ten minutes? Besides, there's nothing left. It looks like an army marched over it."

We stared at it. It reminded me of when we stood looking at those marching monsters in Middleview.

"Wait a minute," I said. "This mess would be perfect to show what the power lines will do to Cranberry Falls, Ethan. All you have to do is put something on the wagon to look like towers and cover that ball of chicken wire with leaves and branches."

"And what do you have to replace my pigeons with, B.J.—Willie?"

I remembered the box hidden under my bed. "Balloons!"

"Balloons?" they all asked.

"They'll be perfect. They say, 'Be prepared for Dorothy Pinkerton to pull down the power lines.' We can blow them up, stick them in with Gerard, and he'll let them go whenever you want, like the pigeons."

"Where did you get them?" asked Kyle.

"Never mind. This is a perfect opportunity to help Mom win the election, like Dad said we should, and still have something to show for the class float."

We pushed what was left of the float out of the barn. The boys hammered wooden poles on the wagon for the towers. Allison cut up the clothesline to use as the connecting wires. I pumped up the balloons and collected some branches.

Ethan was still worried. "We'll have to make signs so they'll know what it is. One of the committee can be a sandwichman and wear the signs on the float."

We were finishing the signs when the committee walked up the driveway. There must have been more than a dozen kids.

"Okay, Eeth," Gerard said. "Where's the float?"

I didn't dare tell him he was standing in front of it.

And even when Ethan did, Gerard wouldn't believe him.

"Come on," he said. "Stop fooling around. There's not much time."

Ethan explained what happened. "It's almost the same idea. You'll be releasing balloons instead of pigeons, that's all, Gerard. Actually, the balloons will be much easier to handle."

"Are you out of your mind?" Gerard screamed. "You really expect me to ride on this monstrosity? I wouldn't be seen anywhere near it. I quit."

"Me too," said another kid. "It stinks. Besides, my parents are Republicans."

The rest of the kids agreed, which seemed pretty rude. Then Gerard and his whole committee walked out the driveway.

"But how will I get the float to the high school?" Ethan shouted.

"Get a horse," Gerard hollered back.

For a few moments nobody spoke. The boys and I stood there looking at Allison.

"I know it's my fault," she finally admitted. "And I'd be happy to let you use Love—honest. But she'd never pull the float without me being there with her."

"You'll be there," said Ethan.

"I will?"

"You just replaced Gerard. Now all I need is someone to wear the signs."

I knew Jon had to save seats for Mom and Dad in the bleachers. And Kyle was playing in the high school band. I was the only one left. I smiled. It was a P.R. person's dream come true.

During the first half of the football game we had to stay hidden with the other floats in the school parking lot. While Allison was complaining inside the chicken wire under all the leaves, I adjusted my signs.

Don't let Cranberry Falls look like this was on my back. The cardboard sign hanging in front said, **Stop the power lines.**

"This thing looks worse than ever," complained Ethan. "Even the branches are wilting."

"That makes it better. Dad says when they put up those high-tension wires, they use dangerous stuff to keep the grass and weeds from growing back. Everything looks dead, like that."

The school band began playing. It was half time and time for the parade.

Smokey the Bear went out on the football field first, with practically the whole senior class pushing it. Next, the juniors shoved this huge American flag made out of flowers onto the field. Then the sophomores hauled their float over behind the juniors. It was the big rocket that Jon said smoke was going to pour out of. He was right. As soon as Love pulled us out onto the field behind them, it started puffing smoke.

"What's on fire?" Allison yelled from under the brush.

MY MOTHER THE MAYOR, MAYBE

"Nothing," I hollered back. I was hoping the applause was for us. But there was so much smoke they couldn't even see us yet.

As we paraded around the field with the other floats, I walked back and forth on the wagon so people could read the signs.

"What's happening?" Allison yelled.

"The band's playing 'Pop goes the Weasel.'"

"I'm not deaf," she shouted. "What's happening, and when can I let the balloons go and get out of here?"

"Two men are standing in front of the band. I think it's the judges."

"I'm sure it is," Ethan called back to us from the wagon seat. "When we pass in front of them, tell Allison to pull the rope that opens my trick door."

We were getting closer to the judges. The bleachers were on one side and the band on the other. I tried to get Kyle's attention, but the boy with the slide trombone kept getting in front of him. I looked over at the bleachers and spotted Mom and Dad with Jon. They were waving like mad at us. Everyone was screaming and throwing streamers all over the place.

I could barely hear Ethan when he shouted, "Now!"

I hurried over to Allison in the clump of branches

and leaves. "Release the balloons," I commanded.

Then I turned to face the judges so they'd be sure to notice my signs. And that's when I saw Mayor Quinn!

I ran back to the wagon seat. "Eeth, it's Mayor Quinn. I don't think he's going to appreciate all this."

"I think you're right. Hold the balloons," said Eeth.

"Hold the balloons," I yelled at Allison under the clump.

But it was too late. Ethan's trick door had worked perfectly. Dozens of balloons were bouncing over the field and into the bleachers. Kids were running and trying to catch them as they landed everywhere. One landed on Mayor Quinn's head. He didn't look very happy when he read what was printed on it.

Then I saw Mom and Dad leaving the bleachers. I had a terrible feeling in the pit of my stomach.

"What's happening?" Allison poked her head through the clump.

"Do you want to change places?" I asked.

She shook her head and disappeared.

The judges signaled all the floats to line up facing the grandstand while the prizes were given out. That was the worst. Especially when I spotted Tony

Spano sitting up there, laughing his fool head off. My P.R. person's dream come true had turned into a nightmare!

The seniors won first prize, the juniors, second, and the sophomores got an honorable mention.

But the freshman class float was the only one that got in the *Courier* that night. I put the picture here in my scrapbook.

That's Mr. Loomis, the school custodian, with the shovel. Love had a little accident. Allison says that's her head coming out of those bushes on the float. It looks more like a balloon to me. That's Ethan sitting there, in the wagon seat, and of course, the horse is Love. Unfortunately, I'm blurred there in the corner of the picture because I was moving. That's Mom and Dad grabbing me off the float. You can see they're upset. In fact, they were furious!

When Dad saw the evening paper, he exploded. "Did you see what they printed under this idiotic picture, Dorothy? 'Kids campaign on campus.' B.J. Pinkerton," he roared, "don't you know it's illegal to campaign on school property?"

"No," I muttered. "I didn't know that. How come Tony Spano passes out buttons and bumper stickers for Mayor Quinn every day in the school cafeteria? He even sells them."

Kids Campaign on Campus

"Well, two wrongs don't make a right," my father the lawyer bellowed.

The phone rang. It was Ethel Grove demanding that Mom call in the balloons because her name wasn't printed on them, too.

"Didn't I tell you I'm part of a team?" Mom snapped at me. "Where did you get those ridiculous balloons?"

"They were a present."

"Oh, good Lord." Dad fell onto the sofa. "Don't you know a candidate cannot accept presents? It might be a bribe."

"It's your fault, Jack. You encouraged her."

"My fault?" Dad yelled at Mom. "That does it! No more publicity, B.J. No more campaigning for any of you kids."

"But you said we should help."

"I also said to stay out of trouble!"

I knew I should have quit politics. But I couldn't. Mr. Shattelles called to remind me the debate with Tony Spano was scheduled for Monday. I'd have to listen to Mom's interview on the radio Sunday whether I wanted to or not.

And then Nancy Tyler called to congratulate me on my great P.R. job. What a friend! She said the balloons looked terrific all over town. She'd even seen one tied to the flagpole at Town Hall.

A P.R. PERSON'S DREAM COME TRUE

"But that's impossible," I said. "There weren't that many."

Nancy giggled. "Uncle Al had a few left over. I told you I'd help your mother win!"

That Nancy was getting out of hand! "Listen, Nancy. Forget trying to help. I'm through with this P.R. business. It's getting me into too much trouble!" I hung up on her.

"I thought you said politics was going to be a wonderful experience," I grumbled at Dad as I went up to bed.

But I couldn't fall asleep. It wasn't because of what happened with the float and balloons either. Something else was bothering me. Something way in the back of my mind, and it wouldn't let me go to sleep. It was those blotters! The blotters with Mom's picture that looked like she was in her underwear. Whatever happened to them? Did Nancy give them back to her Uncle Al to fix? I knew I'd asked her—plenty of times. Come to think of it, she never answered me! And if she dared to climb the flagpole at Town Hall and tie a balloon on top of it, she'd have the nerve to do anything!

I rolled over and buried my face in my pillow. No wonder I couldn't go to sleep. If Mom and Dad blew their stacks over the balloons, what would they do if they ever saw those blotters?

★ ★ 9 ★ ★
I Debate That
Tony Spano

"THE POLITICAL ISSUE chosen as the subject of our debate is, 'Should General Power and Gas be allowed to put high-tension power lines through Cranberry Falls?'" Mr. Shattelles smiled at the class. He was in a good mood for Monday. I guess he figured he could rest up while we talked. He took a coin out of his pants pocket and flipped it, to see who would open the debate. Tony won. He decided he wanted me to go first.

"Each speaker will be given five minutes for his prepared statement," Mr. Shattelles announced.

I DEBATE THAT TONY SPANO

"After B.J. and Tony have presented their points of view, we'll have a rebuttal."

"What's a rebuttal?" someone asked.

"A fight," a boy answered.

"No," Mr. Shattelles corrected him. "It's an opportunity to argue, or to prove your opponent is wrong. Let's begin, shall we? B.J., you're first." Mr. Shattelles leaned back in his chair and smiled again.

I stood in front of the class. I was so nervous, I was shaking.

"Classmates," I began. My voice didn't sound so steady either. "General Power and Gas should not be allowed to put power lines through Cranberry Falls." I looked around the class. Nobody seemed too interested, but at least they weren't asleep. "Power lines will hurt the environment and animals. And the chemicals they use will kill the brush and poison the brooks and the reservoir."

I took one of the maps I'd made and hung it over the blackboard.

"This is where the towers will go." As I drew the line on the map, I had a funny feeling Tony Spano was throwing spitballs in the back of the room.

"Here's where I live." I pointed to Viewland Drive. "See how the towers will cut through the state park? We'll lose our whole lower field and probably have to get rid of our horse, Love. And I'll bet some of you will lose your backyards too."

"Hey, those towers go smack through my living room," some kid shouted.

"They go right through my whole development," another moaned.

"You're right," I told them.

Mr. Shattelles signaled me. I had one minute left.

"Unless something is in your own backyard, it's hard to get involved." While Mr. Shattelles checked his watch, a spitball flew over my head. The class laughed. I finished as quickly as I could. "Well, we'd better get involved because those high-tension wires will soon be in everybody's backyard if we don't fight them. Those power lines are unnecessary, unhealthy, ugly, and most of all, dangerous."

"Time's up!" Mr. Shattelles said.

I walked back to my desk. Tony Spano got me with a spitball, but Nancy winked at me and nodded. And at least a couple of kids clapped—after Nancy got them started.

"Thank you, B.J.," said Mr. Shattelles. "Now let's all be polite and listen to Tony."

Tony walked to the front of the room. He looked ridiculous. He was all dressed up like he was going to church, with a tie on and everything. He took my map off the wall and dropped it to the floor. He grinned at the class and began his stupid speech.

"Friends, don't be fooled. My opponent, B.J. Pinkerton, wants your sympathy because she may lose her horse. Well, don't feel bad. She won't lose that horse because of the power lines and progress. She'll lose that horse because that horse has broken a law. To begin with, the horse was illegally campaigning on your school property Saturday, disguised as part of the Freshman Class Float. That horse insulted our mayor, who was one of the judges, and deliberately destroyed the float by eating it."

"It was an accident," I yelled at him. "And how about you, selling buttons for Mayor Quinn in the cafeteria!"

"Quiet! Watch the rules, B.J.," Mr. Shattelles said. "And stick to the subject, Tony."

Tony smirked and continued. "All right. Maybe it was an accident. But is breaking a zoning law an accident? We have a law in our town that prohibits keeping a horse on your property unless you have at least five acres. The Pinkertons have four."

"So what?" my friend Nancy hollered from her desk. "You told us that before. Besides, one horse doesn't need five acres. In Middleview, they only need three acres."

I tried to sit very still and not bite all my nails off. How could I hate anyone so much?

"I ask you," that nut went on, "shouldn't a candidate for the highest office in Cranberry Falls set an example for the other citizens by at least obeying the laws?"

Mr. Shattelles looked at his watch. "One minute left, Tony. And please, get off the subject of horses and on to the power lines."

The class giggled.

"Yes, sir." Tony glanced at his notes and adjusted his father's necktie. "For one horse, are you going to deprive all those people in the cities of their right to have energy, just because B.J. Pinkerton may lose her lower field, and the horse won't have a place to graze? I'm certain our government will protect us from any poisonous chemicals General Power and Gas, or any utility company, might mistakenly use. Fellow classmates, the Pinkertons shouldn't have a horse on that property in the first place. It's illegal, and they should be fined. *That* horse has to go."

The class didn't applaud very much for Tony either. A few booed.

"Let's remember our manners," Mr. Shattelles warned. "Quiet down."

The boos made me feel good. The class wasn't that

dumb. They knew Tony Spano was trying to avoid the real issue. But I wished he'd stop talking about Allison's horse and that zoning law.

"Now for the rebuttal period." Mr. Shattelles nodded at me. "Two minutes, B.J."

I guess I shouldn't have brought up the subject of the election, but I couldn't help it. "You'd better tell your parents to vote for Dorothy Pinkerton," I told them all. "She realizes there are other ways to get power to those cities, if they really need it. Think of all the animals that will be hurt by those chemicals— and people may be hurt too. Think how the noise those wires make buzzing will hurt your ears. Save our animals. Save our land for them. Remember. We don't have to let them put those high-tension wires over our heads. Power lines can go underground. Vote for Pinkerton. Thank you."

As I sat down the applause wasn't tremendous, but it was more than Tony got. Nancy even began yelling and stamping her feet. I felt wonderful, not only because I didn't have to say anymore but because what Mom said about politics was true. It made you care about more than just yourself, and that was a good feeling.

"Now, let's have order, please," shouted Mr. Shattelles. "Give Tony his two minutes for rebuttal."

Tony Spano walked to the front of the classroom with a large piece of paper rolled under his arm.

"Fellow classmates, I didn't want to stoop so low and make this debate personal. But as long as my opponent, Ms. Pinkerton, has brought up the name of her mother, and my father is campaign manager for the Republicans, I think I have the right to ask for equal time and tell you that your parents should vote for Mayor Quinn." Tony walked over to the blackboard. "Any candidate that allows publicity like this doesn't deserve to be mayor." Then, right where I had hung my map, Tony stuck this huge piece of paper and began unrolling it. "Does this person have the dignity to be mayor of Cranberry Falls?"

You could hear the class gasp!

I couldn't move. I sat there, at my desk, staring at this enlarged picture of my mother in the top of her bathing suit. The one on the blotter. It wasn't only the picture, it was the whole blotter, enlarged one hundred times. And the bathing suit looked more like underwear than ever!

The class was laughing. Some boys even began whistling.

Mr. Shattelles started banging on his desk and hollering, "Order! Order!"

I turned and looked at Nancy. She looked away. I

knew then she'd never collected the blotters or taken them back to her Uncle Al to fix. She probably even left one in Tony Spano's mailbox that day she got them. And I'll bet his big, smart-aleck brother, Joe, enlarged it in the high school darkroom.

Mr. Shattelles couldn't stop the noise. Some kids grabbed Mom's picture and paraded around the room holding it over their heads. Then the whole class was marching around, laughing and throwing things.

"Nobody wins this debate," Mr. Shattelles yelled. An eraser hit him on the nose. "You both lose," he roared.

I thought I was going to be sick. I got up and walked out of the classroom.

"B.J., B.J. Pinkerton, come back here," I heard Mr. Shattelles calling.

But I kept walking, down the hall and out the front door of the Middle School.

And then I started running, running as fast as I could. My eyes got all watery and everything was blurred. I didn't know where I was going, and I didn't care. I only knew I never wanted to see Nancy Tyler or Tony Spano again as long as I lived.

★ ★ 10 ★ ★

The Bad Guys

I DON'T KNOW WHY I headed for the old railroad
station. Maybe I was thinking so crazy I hoped by a
miracle the trains had started running there again and
I could get out of town, fast. I guess I went there
because I knew it would be empty until three o'clock,
and I knew where the key was. At least I could hide
there in the waiting room until things straightened
out in my head.

I was right. Campaign headquarters was deserted.
There wasn't a person in sight. I stood on the

window sill and reached behind the **All Aboard with the Democrats** sign above the door. The key fell off the ledge. I jumped down and put it in the keyhole.

There were benches against the walls in the tiny waiting room. I wanted to throw myself down on one. But I was afraid someone might pass by and look through the windows. So I went inside the small ticket-taker's office where no one could see me and sat on the floor.

Every time I tried to think about the debate and Tony Spano and Nancy not taking the blotters back, I hurt so much inside I could hardly breathe. And if I closed my eyes, all I could see was that picture of Mom in her bathing suit top that looked like a bra. And when I tried not to cry, everything hurt even more. So I decided I might as well cry and get it over with. Once I started, I couldn't stop.

I must have fallen asleep, because the next thing I knew, I heard a man talking.

"Someone left the key in the door."

Then I noticed the smell. I recognized it right away, like I can tell the smell of Mom's stew or the boys' sneakers. It was Mr. Jessup's cigar. I could see the smoke above me, coming right through the ticket-taker's window.

"That's strange," he was saying. "The volunteers

never open headquarters during the week until three in the afternoon."

Then he practically scared me to death. "Anybody here?" he shouted.

His footsteps were coming closer. Oh, my gosh. What if he finds me? How can I explain?

"Nobody's here, Sam."

It was Charlie Knots! I could tell that mean voice anywhere.

"Somebody probably stopped by to pick up some campaign literature," he continued, "and forgot to lock the door. Maybe I'd better order a little more."

So Charlie Knots did have something to do with that awful literature! I thought so.

Sam Jessup was laughing. "Don't order any more unless you get a new printer. Who prints that stuff anyway?"

"My brother," Charlie howled.

"Shh, control yourself, Charlie," Mr. Jessup said.

It's funny how I knew they were going to start talking about Mom, just like they did that night I got caught on the stairs and that Charlie ate Willie's dog food. But I was too scared to say anything. Besides, I had a feeling if they knew I was sitting on the floor in the ticket office with only a piece of plywood between us, I'd be a goner.

"Be serious, Charlie," Mr. Jessup was saying. "There's only one week before the election. That Pinkerton woman has made such a commotion over those power lines, Mayor Quinn has got to take a stand, one way or the other."

"What do you mean, Sam?" Boy, that Charlie was stupid! Even I knew what Sam Jessup meant.

"The mayor wasn't strong enough on that radio interview. He's going to have to say the power lines are necessary and prove it," Mr. Jessup said, "or agree with the Democrats and stop the power lines."

"Wait a minute, Sam," said Charlie Knots. "Myron's a Republican. He can't agree with the Democrats. But if he says the power lines are necessary and he can't prove it, won't that look bad?"

"You bet," agreed Sam Jessup. "And he'll lose the election for sure."

"Don't be ridiculous, Sam. Nobody wants a woman for mayor. Didn't I resign and quit the race so Dorothy Pinkerton could step into my shoes and Myron Quinn wouldn't have any competition?"

But the *Courier* said Charlie Knots had quit the race because of ill health!

"You'd better listen to me, Charlie." Mr. Jessup wasn't very happy. "Meet Your Candidates night is this Thursday. The League of Women Voters is

getting the whole town out. Everyone will be there.
Dorothy Pinkerton is going to talk about stopping
those power lines. The mayor better have something
worth listening to, or—" he paused.

"Or what?" asked Charlie.

"Or he won't be mayor anymore."

"Stop talking like that, Sam." Charlie sounded real
loud and mean. "The only reason I quit the race for
mayor was because you told me General Power and
Gas was planning to put those power lines through
my ten acres. You said I could make a lot of money."

Charlie Knots was never sick at all. Too bad. But
what did Charlie's ten acres have to do with the
power lines?

"I only did what you asked me to, Charlie," Sam
Jessup said. "I took you off the ballot and put
Dorothy Pinkerton on in your place so that you could
bargain with General Power and Gas. You knew if
you were elected mayor and they wanted to buy your
property, it might be a conflict of interest. It
wouldn't look right. I never dreamed a silly woman
would make an issue of those power lines and spoil
everything."

"She's not going to spoil anything! We've got to
see to it that Myron Quinn gets reelected and those
power lines go through."

THE BAD GUYS

Charlie Knots was acting exactly like one of those bad guys on television. Only this was really happening, and he meant every word he said!

"You're right," Sam Jessup told Charlie. "We've both got too much to lose."

"What do you mean, Sam? All you've got to lose is a promise from Myron that he'll try to get you a job at Town Hall. If those power lines don't go through Cranberry Falls, I'll lose everything!"

"You won't *lose* a thing, Charlie. You just won't *get* anything."

I heard the door open and close. I was trembling so much I could hardly stand up. I peeked through the ticket window. The waiting room was empty, so I ran out of the ticket office and headed for the door. I couldn't believe what I suspected was really the truth. Sam Jessup and Charlie Knots were in cahoots with Mayor Quinn, and they were all out to get Mom!

I reached for the doorknob.

I'd better wait, I thought. I can't let those bad guys know I heard them talking. They'll get rid of me on the spot, like on that television show. I'd better give them time to get down the street.

I ducked back away from the window and went over to a bench. I noticed one of my **Vote for Pinkerton** signs hanging upside down on the wall.

Charlie Knots did that, I'll bet. I straightened it and sat down.

As Mom's P.R. person, hadn't I seen right through those two? I knew all along they'd ruined the campaign literature on purpose. And now I knew why Jessup didn't want Mom to talk about the power lines. They weren't on our side at all. They never had been. The whole election was fixed so that Mom would lose, even from the beginning.

I had to get home and tell Mom and Dad everything.

I ran to the door. Wait a minute—tell them everything? Even about the debate with Tony Spano and the blotter with Mom's picture? The blotter my *ex*-friend Nancy Tyler was probably distributing all over town. They hadn't gotten over the balloons yet, and I was supposed to stay out of trouble.

I took a deep breath and decided. This was more important than any old blotter. When Mom understood how fishy everything was, she wouldn't have time to be angry. She'd be too busy "blotting out" the Republicans. Trouble was, she'd have to "blot out" a few Democrats too.

I glanced out the window. The coast was clear. I turned the knob. Darn it. The door was stuck. I pulled real hard. It still wouldn't budge. It was locked! Mr. Jessup had locked the door and put the key back up on the ledge—outside!

I hurried over to the side door and yanked that knob. It came off in my hand. My heart began thumping like crazy.

I looked around the waiting room. What a relief. There were telephones in the corner—the ones Mom had told us about. The Democrats had installed them so the districts could call in the results on election night. I could phone Dad at his office. He'd come over and get me out of this place.

But when I lifted the receiver, there wasn't a sound. The phones hadn't been hooked up yet.

There was only one thing left to do. Go out the window! It had to be the side window, though, above a bench and I'd have to hurry so no one would see me climbing out.

I ran across the room and jumped up on the bench. I had to stand on my tiptoes to see out the window. How could it be so high up and far from the ground when it was only the first floor?

But I could make it—especially if I went out backward, feet first. I wished I had my jeans on, instead of the stupid skirt I'd worn for the debate.

I shoved open the window and climbed up onto the ledge. I put my legs out. Then I twisted myself around and held on to the window sill. As I lowered myself almost to the ground, I heard my skirt ripping. Darn. It was caught on a nail and I was stuck. I had to shimmy up a bit and unhook it.

The next thing I knew, someone grabbed me from behind. I was too scared to look around! If it was those bad guys, I was a goner! I opened my mouth to scream.

"You're under arrest," a voice said.

Then I heard a little click, like a camera.

I turned and looked. I was being held by the police!

No wonder Cyrilla Cornsby never got promoted beyond the society column. She never went to work. She was always snooping around taking pictures. And I don't know what the police were doing cruising down Main Street in the middle of the day, wasting gas.

"Why, it's B.J. Pinkerton," Cyrilla practically yelled. She was taking her pad and pencil out of her pocketbook. "Why aren't you in school, B.J.?"

"Breaking and entering, or leaving?" the officer said as he set me on the ground.

I looked at him. Was he serious? Or just making believe?

While I was trying to decide, another policeman

stepped out of the patrol car and walked over to Cyrilla. "Wait a minute, Miss. We gotta give this person her rights."

The officer holding on to me was saying something about me having the right to remain silent because anything I said could be held against me.

"And you have the right to have a lawyer," interrupted the other officer. "If you can't afford one, the court will appoint one for you."

I gulped. They were probably kidding me, but I wasn't taking any chances. "I demand a lawyer," I said, just like I heard on that television show. "And would you mind driving me home—to his house?"

★ ★ 11 ★ ★

"Whose Side Are You On, Anyway?"

IT WAS TERRIBLE. The siren was wailing and the police car was speeding up Main Street. Everyone turned around to look. What if they recognized me? My father would have a fit.

Everything will be all right as soon as you get home, I told myself. I covered my ears and crouched down on the floor.

I couldn't escape even if I tried. I was like an animal, caught in one of Ethan's Havahart traps. There were no handles on the inside of the back doors. And there was a screen between me and the two policemen in the front seat.

I remembered in third grade when the teacher took us to visit the police station. I thought it would be wonderful to ride in a police car with the sirens wailing. It wasn't wonderful at all. It was awful.

Fortunately, my lawyer was home for lunch. He and Mom must have heard the siren. They ran out to the back porch as the police car drove in the driveway. They were in a state of shock, seeing me delivered to the door that way.

Unfortunately, they were expecting me. Mr. Shattelles had telephoned from school that I was missing—and by the looks on their faces, he must have told them why.

I didn't want to mention the bad guys until I spoke privately with my lawyer. So I said I'd locked myself in the railroad station and that the police had caught me climbing out the window.

"B.J.'s a volunteer worker for the Democrats," Mom said.

"So of course she wasn't illegally breaking into the headquarters," Dad told the officers. "And I'll let the school know she's safe at home."

"We knew she'd get a kick out of riding in the police car. Right, B.J.?" said one of the officers.

Both officers laughed.

"Right." I tried to smile. I would have enjoyed the ride more if they'd told me they were kidding in the first place.

The police left. Thank goodness, they didn't start that siren again!

Dad marched me inside and sat me down on the sofa in the keeping room. He began questioning me, like I was on trial or something!

"Who locked you in the railroad station, young lady?"

"Huh? How did you know?"

"That old door at headquarters has to be opened and locked with a key."

Boy, my father's not only a lawyer, he's a detective, too.

"I thought I told you to stay out of trouble. What's this about a picture at school of your mother wearing—"

"Wait!" I stopped him. "First, let me tell you about the bad guys."

"Bad guys?"

"What are you talking about, B.J.?" Mom sat down next to me.

That's when I told the whole truth, about Nancy and the blotters and the debate with Tony. And I told them how I got stuck in the railroad station and heard those bad guys talking, and how scared I was when I found out I was locked in.

Dad sat on the arm of the sofa. "But there really isn't anything wrong with what those two said, B.J. There's nothing 'fishy' going on, believe me. Jessup and Knots and Quinn have been friends all their lives. I told you that before. Just because they belong to different political parties doesn't mean they can't be friends."

"Charlie Knots was supposed to be sick," I said. "What about that conflict of interest?"

"Charlie Knots was smart enough to know he shouldn't get involved and run for mayor if he wanted to sell his land to General Power and Gas. He didn't run, and so there's no conflict of interest. It's as simple as that!" Dad walked over to get his jacket off the armchair. "Now I want you to stop all this publicity stuff. And this time, I mean it!"

Mom stood up. "Well, I think B.J. is right. They shouldn't be talking like that behind my back. I don't care if they have been friends for years. Sam Jessup and Charlie Knots are Democrats. They're supposed to be trying to get me elected mayor of Cranberry Falls, not trying to keep their Republican friend, Myron Quinn, in office forever."

"All right, what do you want me to do about it? Sam Jessup and Charlie Knots *are* Democrats. It certainly wouldn't do your campaign any good to have members of your own party investigated. Besides, they haven't done anything wrong."

Mom was furious. She walked right over to Dad and grabbed his arm. "I didn't want to run in the first place. You're the one who encouraged me and found out about the power lines. And you're the one who decided we should all get out there and campaign."

"I didn't think you'd stay out there campaigning twenty-four hours a day," Dad shouted at her. "You can't think about anything but running for mayor. You've completely forgotten you have a family, and a husband who would like something to eat besides hot dogs once in a while."

"Whose side are you on, anyway?" Mom shouted back at Dad.

"You're as confused as B.J. You're getting so involved you can't see the woods for the trees." Dad pulled his jacket on. "It's not the end of the world. It will all be over in a week, and you can come home and start being a wife and mother again."

There was an awful silence. My father walked toward the kitchen.

Mom didn't move. "You think being a wife and

mother means staying home all the time?"

"I didn't say that."

"You think I don't have a chance, don't you?"

"I didn't say that either."

"You don't want me to win—any more than Sam Jessup or Charlie Knots does."

"Dorothy, of course I do, but—"

Mom waited for Dad to continue. So did I. It was so quiet I could hear Willie's nails clicking on the linoleum in the kitchen.

"But I miss you, and so do the kids."

"Is that true, B.J.?"

"Well—" I wasn't sure what I was supposed to say. Mom was a wife and mother like Dad said, but she shouldn't have to stay home all the time. But I did miss her when she was at those meetings every night. And what would it be like if she was elected mayor, maybe for eighteen years, like Myron Quinn?

"Of course, B.J. misses you," Dad said. "None of us realized how much of your time this campaign would take."

Mom didn't say anything.

Dad walked through the kitchen to the back door. I could see him taking his briefcase off the counter. He looked back at us. "Maybe if you were home a little more, Dorothy, your daughter wouldn't be skipping school and getting picked up by the police!" He started out the door and stopped. "And maybe your husband wouldn't have to go to the local diner for something to eat because you forgot to give him lunch!"

The door slammed.

Mom waited a minute, but when she spoke, her voice sounded funny, like she had a cold or something. "Have I been neglecting you, B.J., and the rest of the family?"

I jumped up and hugged her. "Of course not," I told her. She had enough to worry about. "Everything is fine. Don't worry. I'll get back those blotters from Nancy, and I won't get in any more trouble. I promise. I won't even campaign."

"Don't you dare stop campaigning, B.J." Mom almost sounded angry at me! "I'll need every bit of help I can get."

"Huh?"

"I've decided I want very much to be mayor, and I'm going to fight to win." Mom got her coat and hat out of the closet and headed for the door. "I'll go see Mr. Shattelles now, and take care of that blotter. Then I have to drop in on a few 'coffees' Ethel Grove has set up. I won't be home until late because I'm speaking at the Chamber of Commerce dinner."

"That's okay," I said.

Mom kissed me on the cheek. Willie was standing at the door, trembling from listening to all that arguing. She stopped and petted him. "At least I know you're on my side, Willie."

"I am too," I told her. "It's too bad neither one of us can vote."

Mom ran out to the car. "There's still some hot dogs left in the freezer," she called as she drove off.

I went back into the keeping room and collapsed on the sofa. Willie jumped up and curled next to me.

"Politics sure does strange things to people, Willie. Look what it's done to those bad guys—Jessup, Knots, and Quinn. And look what politics has done to my ex-friend Nancy Tyler—made her steal that picture and lie about those blotters! My mother is acting like she's possessed, and my father can't think straight anymore. Did you ever hear them fight like that before?"

Willie groaned and rolled over as I scratched his stomach.

"Even I'm acting funny since we got into politics, Willie, imagining all those crazy things. There's only one person who hasn't changed—Tony Spano. He's as much a jerk now as he was before!"

When the boys and Allison got home from school, I told them what had happened.

"They'll probably get a divorce," moaned Allison.

"People in politics are always getting divorced. What's happening to this family?"

"It's falling apart," said Ethan.

Allison moaned some more. "I'm losing my parents, my horse, everything."

"Well, you wanted to move into the White House," Jon reminded her.

"Are you certain you're not imagining all this, B.J.?" Kyle asked. "Nobody gets along better than Mom and Dad."

"Not anymore. He doesn't even want her to win, Kyle."

"Of course he does, stupid. He just misses her, like we all do."

"But what if she wins, and she's never home?" I asked.

"It'll be rotten," said Ethan.

"Yeah," agreed Jon, "especially if Allison's the cook."

"Don't worry," Allison said. "I'm not going to waste my life cooking and cleaning for all of you like Mom has. Nobody is going to make me stay home!"

"You're as spoiled as Willie, Allison Pinkerton," I told her. "Mom's always been home, cooking and doing everything for Dad and all of us. Now for once she wants something, to be mayor. And all we're thinking about is ourselves."

"You haven't been much help, getting in all that trouble with those balloons and now some blotters," Allison said.

"You're both spoiled," piped up Ethan.

"Listen, everybody," Kyle raised his voice. "I make a motion that we campaign for Mom every minute from now on."

"So she'll know we believe in her," added Allison.

"There could be an upset," said Jon. "Remember, every vote counts, and we've still got a whole week."

"But Dad said to stop all the publicity stuff," I told them.

"Don't worry," said Ethan. "When Dad comes to his senses, he'll start campaigning again, too."

"Well, I know I'll do anything to beat those Republicans," said Allison.

"Good," I said. "You can give free rides on Love to every kid who promises his parents will vote for Mom."

"What are you talking about? I said, *I'd* do anything. That does *not* include my horse."

"Wait a minute, that's a great idea, B.J.," said Kyle. "If you did it soon, Al, like maybe Wednesday after school at headquarters, it could mean a lot of votes for Mom."

"Everyone will realize what a great horse Love is,"

I said, "and sign a petition making the town change the zoning law so that you can keep your horse."

"What petition?"

"The one we could circulate while you're giving the free rides."

"Well . . ." she paused.

"And I'll bet Cyrilla Cornsby will be there taking pictures," I added.

That did it! "I'll think about it," said Allison.

The phone rang. Willie started biting the sofa pillows. I ran to answer.

It was Nancy. She was calling to find out if we were still best friends.

"Best friends?" I hollered at her. "I was locked in the railroad station and got arrested. My father may divorce my mother. My whole family is breaking up. It's all your fault. And you want to be best friends?"

"You got arrested?"

"Practically."

"I'm really sorry, B.J. I don't know how Tony got the blotter. I thought I collected the ones I passed out."

"What happened to the others?" I had to wait a long time before Nancy said anything.

"I never gave them back to Uncle Al at all. He was so proud of the good job he did, I couldn't hurt his feelings like that. We can still use them, B.J. We could cut the picture off. Half a blotter is better than none. Please say you'll forgive me."

"I don't know, Nancy. You really messed things up."

"But I got the enlarged picture and we burned it."

"You burned it?"

"Yup, half the class and me. We took it out on the football field, and we burned it. I would have called sooner, but I had to stay after. The principal thought we were trying to set the school on fire."

I decided anyone who would risk burning down the school couldn't be that bad. "I forgive you, Nancy."

"I don't want you just to forgive me, B.J. I want you to say I'm still your best friend."

"Nancy, you can't expect me to get over what happened today in a few hours. Maybe next week you'll be my best friend."

"It's a deal! And wait until you see the surprise I've got for you!"

"Forget it, Nancy. I really don't want any more surprises. But there's a big Meet Your Candidates night this Thursday. And Wednesday, something fantastic is going to happen at the railroad station. We may need some help."

"You've got it," my friend Nancy said.

★ ★ 12 ★ ★
Joshua Cranberry
Rides Again!

By Wednesday afternoon, Nancy and I had plastered our signs all over. And every kid in school had promised to come. Every kid except Tony Spano.

"I'm manning the Republican headquarters every day after school," he bragged.

Allison had already left. She was riding her horse to the station.

Kyle had permission to drive the rest of us downtown.

I was sitting in the car with the boys, waiting for Nancy.

A deliveryman stopped out front. "Package for B.J. Pinkerton," he shouted.

"For me?" I jumped out of the car.

It *was* for me! But who would be sending me a package? I was about to open it when I remembered what Nancy said. It might be a bomb! What if those bad guys, Jessup and Knots, found out I'd heard them talking and wanted to get rid of me? I wasn't going to take any chances.

I ran over to the side of the house and grabbed the hose. Then I squirted water all over the box, like Nancy said I should. It sure smelled funny—like a bomb, all right.

I was going to open the box but Nancy came pedaling up the driveway.

Kyle honked the horn. "Nancy's here. Let's get going, B.J." He started the car.

Nancy left her bicycle against the tree. I ran over with the box.

"This just arrived," I told her. "I soaked it though, like you said I should. It could be a bomb."

Nancy didn't look too happy. "It could be my surprise."

"What surprise?"

"The bumper stickers I ordered for you. There's a thousand in that box."

"No!"

"And I personally donated the whole thousand," sighed Nancy.

"I ruined them," I groaned.

We tore open the box. No wonder it smelled. It was the glue. The stickers were all stuck together.

"What do they say?" I asked Nancy as I tried to pull one out.

"Well, there's a picture of Town Hall. Next to it is printed, 'Bump out Mayor Quinn . . . Bump Dorothy Pinkerton in.'"

"That's beautiful, Nancy."

Kyle honked the horn, again. "If you two don't come this minute, we're leaving without you."

I was going to dump the box behind the back porch in the garbage, but I didn't have the heart. Nancy looked so sad that I couldn't throw the bumper stickers away.

"We'll take them to headquarters with us," I said. "Maybe we can stick them somewhere while they're still wet so that it won't be a total loss."

Kyle was driving out the driveway!

"Wait for us," I yelled as we ran for the car.

It looked like a three-ring circus outside the railroad station. And Allison looked like the ringmaster, standing in the middle of this huge circle the boys had roped off after they cleared the old parking lot.

She was wearing her riding outfit and a top hat we'd found in the attic. The best was the training whip she pretended to use and the black mustache she got off an old Halloween mask. She'd taped it under her nose.

She was holding a long lunge line she had hitched to Love's bridle. Love was prancing around the ring with these big paper ears Nancy and I had tied over her own so she'd look more like the Democratic donkey than a backyard horse.

"Cyrilla Cornsby's going to love it. And you'll get your reward for being so generous," I promised Allison. "You'll be on the front page of the *Courier,* wait and see."

"I'd better be. That's part of the bargain, remember?" Allison picked up what looked like a large cardboard funnel.

"What's that?"

"My megaphone," she said and began shouting into it. "Get your free rides on gentle, lovely Love and vote for Dorothy Pinkerton."

The place was mobbed. While Ethan sold popcorn, and Jon and Kyle kept the kids in line waiting for their rides, Nancy and I got the parents to sign the petition.

As long as there was such a crowd, I decided to pass out some campaign literature. I had to use that stuff Charlie Knots had printed with Mom's horrible picture. Before I handed it out, I wrote *Pinkerton* across Mom's face so they'd remember the name and forget the face.

Nancy kept checking the box of bumper stickers in the car. "We've got to do something quick," she said. "They're drying out."

"If only there was some place nearby to put them," I said.

We both looked across the street at the same time and said it together. "The Republican headquarters!"

The beautiful glass storefront was perfect!

"And everybody's over here. There's no one over there," said Nancy.

"Except Tony Spano," I reminded her.

"Just get him to come over for a free ride," said Nancy. "I'll take care of the bumper stickers."

"He'll never come."

"He would if you asked him. He can't resist you, B.J."

"Me? Ask Tony Spano to ride my sister's horse? The horse he's been campaigning against for weeks?

Are you out of your mind? My sister wouldn't let him get near her horse, and I wouldn't stoop so low as to ask him."

"You want your mother to win, don't you?"

"Of course."

"And she needs the publicity. My father says, sometimes you have to make sacrifices, especially in politics."

"Well—"

"And what about me? I already sacrificed my whole year's allowance. Those bumper stickers were expensive."

I looked across the street. I could see Tony Spano now. He was standing in one of the huge store windows pretending he was putting up another picture of Mayor Quinn. Actually, he was watching everything that was going on.

"If he does come over," I said, "he'll lock the door."

"I won't have to go inside. I'll stick them on the outside of the windows."

"But, once you stick those things on, aren't they hard to get off?" I asked Nancy.

"That's the point," she replied.

I thought about how much Mom wanted to be mayor.

"Okay," I said. "But first you have to warn Allison and explain. Otherwise, she won't let him on the horse. Then, while I'm in the Republican headquarters, get the bumper stickers out of the car. When you see me crossing the street with Tony, get to work."

Everything had to be timed perfectly.

I walked up and down the sidewalk in front of the railroad station, passing out more literature.

As soon as I saw Nancy talking to Allison, I waved at Tony. He looked surprised. I forced myself to smile at him. Talk about sacrifices! He waved and smiled back. I braced myself and crossed the street.

The minute I walked into his headquarters, I could tell Tony was suspicious. He didn't say a word. I could see Nancy running over to the car for the bumper stickers. I had to talk fast and make it sound good. It wasn't easy, but I knew exactly what I had to say.

"Just because we belong to different political parties doesn't mean we can't be friends, Tony. How about a free ride on Allison's horse?"

Nancy was wrong. Tony Spano could resist me. He shook his head and stood looking out the window. Then Cyrilla Cornsby arrived with her camera. It was Cyrilla and the camera he couldn't resist!

"Okay." He grinned. "I'll be a good sport. What difference does it make? I've got to lock up, though."

"Of course," I said. I could see Nancy waiting behind the big maple tree next to the station. She was holding the box.

I walked across the street with Tony and over to the ring. Allison was posing with her horse for Cyrilla. As soon as she saw us, she picked up her megaphone.

"Ladies and gentlemen, it is my pleasure to present to you the world's greatest rider, Tony Spano."

That stupid Tony couldn't even get on the horse. Allison had to help him get on by giving him a leg up. Then he started showing off.

"What do you think I am, a baby?" he asked Allison. "I can ride by myself. You don't have to lead me."

"I think I'd better," said Allison, smiling at Cyrilla.

Tony leaned forward to unsnap the lunge line. "Take this thing away. I don't need it."

"Well, if you're sure it's what you want," Allison said, removing the line. Then she took the training whip from under her arm and gave Love a little tap on her backside.

Love took off like a streak of lightning.

"Hold on to the reins," Allison yelled as Love

jumped over the ropes and galloped off behind the station. She went so fast Cyrilla didn't even have time to take a picture. And how Tony Spano managed to hang on, I'll never know. But he did—for a while, anyway.

"Aren't you going to try to stop her?" I asked Allison.

"Love knows exactly what she's doing, and I know exactly where she's going."

Allison was right. That horse was headed for the old cornfields near the brook behind Town Hall. Everyone was shouting and laughing at Tony—and clapping too. That clown never should have turned back to smile and wave at everybody. Because when Love reached the edge of the cornfield, she stopped to eat a few ears left on an old stalk. Tony slid off the horse and landed in the brook.

"Joshua Cranberry rides again!" sighed Allison as she picked up her megaphone. "And don't be alarmed, folks. Gentle, lovely Love has taken a few moments off for a little snack, and Tony's not hurt. They'll be back in a moment and your free rides will continue. Meanwhile, don't forget to sign our petition."

I was about to check to see how Nancy was doing. I didn't have to. She was standing next to me.

"I used every one," she whispered.

I looked over at the Republican headquarters. She sure did. The windows had disappeared. All you could see were Mom's bumper stickers.

I pointed over to the cornfields where Love was eating the corn and Tony was standing in the brook, wringing out his jacket. "It worked perfectly," I told Nancy.

Then I saw Mr. Jessup. He was hurrying down the sidewalk toward us. I could tell by the look on his face that something was wrong.

"What's going on?" he asked, shoving everyone around. "Who's in charge of this fiasco?"

"We're giving free rides to everyone who votes for Mom," I told him.

He shook that terrible cigar at me. "Young lady, you're buying votes, and that's illegal. What do you want to do, get us all in jail? Who do you think you are?"

Before I could remind him that he was the one who had given me permission to be Mom's P.R. person, he was ordering the boys to take down the ropes and sending all the people home, including Cyrilla.

I was never so mad in my whole life. I knew he was stopping us because he didn't want Mom to win.

And there wasn't a thing we could do.

"At least we got rid of the bumper stickers and got the signatures for the petition," Nancy said.

"And don't forget," said Allison, "Cyrilla took my picture. I'll probably be on the front page of the *Courier,* and that will be great publicity for Mom." She took off her mustache and ran to get Love out of the cornfield.

Tony Spano had disappeared.

A car with a huge sign stuck on the roof pulled up in front of the station. **Vote for My Dorothy** was printed on the sign.

"It's your father," shouted Nancy.

"He must have come to his senses," I told her as we ran to the sidewalk. "He's campaigning for Mom again."

"Gosh, Mr. Pinkerton, your car looks great," Nancy told Dad.

"Come on, I'll take you both home," he said.

We hopped in.

"Wait until you see what I did to the picket fence." The car pulled away from the curb. "There's a sign so big that it completely covers—"

My father almost ran into the telephone pole. "Who—who did that?" He pointed to the Republican's storefront.

Before I could confess, he stopped me.

"Don't say a word. Forget I asked. I don't want to know anything about it. All I can say is, I wish *I'd* thought of it."

As we drove off, I looked back. Tony was standing in the street outside the Republican headquarters, yelling. It's a good thing we couldn't hear what he was saying!

★ ★ 13 ★ ★

"Win or Lose..."

WE WERE HAVING an early dinner so the whole family could go over to the high school together. That's where the League of Women Voters was having their important Meet Your Candidates night.

As soon as we sat down, the phone rang.

"Don't move, Mom." I jumped up to get it. "Save yourself for your speech."

It was Nancy. "Have you seen the newspaper, Beej?"

"It's not here yet. Why?"

"You made the front page."

"Me? It's supposed to be Allison and her horse. Are you sure it's me?"

"Well, you can't see much of your face, but your name's under the picture. It says—"

"Never mind," I interrupted her. Through the window I could see Tony Spano bicycling up the drive. "The paper just arrived. The enemy is throwing it on the porch."

I ran outside.

Tony was sitting on his bike, waiting for me. He sneezed. "You think you're funny, don't you?" He sneezed again.

Maybe he caught a cold in the brook! "What do you mean?" I said.

"You know what I mean. But I'll get the last laugh tonight when I sell the *Courier* at the high school." He began to laugh. "Your old lady hasn't got a chance, B.J." He laughed all the way down the driveway. He was laughing so hard I thought for sure he'd fall off his bike and land on his head again, like he did when he fell off the horse. I watched him coast down the hill, hoping he would, but he didn't.

I picked up the newspaper. I took one look and wanted to die. Nancy was right about the picture. It was me—all over the front page.

How could I have been so stupid and forgotten

Cyrilla was at the railroad station Monday? And how could Cyrilla Cornsby have been so mean and given the *Courier* that picture of me climbing out the station house window backwards, with the policeman waiting below to arrest me?

No wonder Tony was laughing. In the picture it looks like my skirt is half off. The other half is hanging up there on that nail on the window sill. It was so humiliating I couldn't even cut it out of the newspaper. I did put what it said under the picture in my scrapbook. You can read that:

B.J. Pinkerton Turns Campaign into Three-Ring Circus.

I felt like I did after the debate. Ashamed—and mad at everybody, especially myself. I wanted to run away again too. But this time, I couldn't. There was no place to go. Besides, what good would it do? I'd still have to face everyone eventually and explain everything, same as before. But what awful publicity for my mother!

When I got up enough courage, I went inside and showed Mom and everybody the picture.

Nobody said much except Allison.

"I thought I was the one who was supposed to be on the front page," she complained. "How come I'm way back on page thirty-seven, and why didn't you

"WIN OR LOSE . . ."

tell me no one would recognize me with that black mustache all over my face?"

It was time to go to the high school, but I told them I wasn't going. "Tony Spano will be at the door, passing out that newspaper to everyone who comes," I cried.

"So what?" said Jon.

"Everyone will laugh."

"Yesterday everyone laughed at Tony, and you didn't worry about that," Kyle reminded me.

"B.J., this is the most important time in the whole campaign," Mom said. "I need you there to support me."

"You can't quit now, B.J." Dad said.

"You can wear my black mustache so no one will recognize you," offered Allison.

I knew they were right and that I had to go. Thank goodness, Ethan rescued me.

"Just go and stand backstage," he said.

The auditorium was packed. I was standing offstage in the wings where no one could see me. I peeked around the clump of curtains. Dad and Allison and the boys were sitting in the front row. I could see Nancy wandering in the back of the auditorium, looking for me. Mrs. Duby, the president of the League of Women Voters, had finished introducing all the candidates. Mr. Spano was way over on the other side of the stage with Mayor Quinn and the Republicans. Mom, Mr. Jessup, and the Democrats were on the side closer to me. I had to admit it was a perfect place to see everything.

Mrs. Duby flipped a coin, just like Mr. Shattelles had done for our debate, and then she sat down on a chair in the middle of the stage near the microphone and smiled.

I watched Mom walk over to the microphone and stand in front of it. She looked lovely. Her hair had grown a bit longer so it didn't look bushy, like Mayor Quinn's, anymore. She began speaking.

I never realized what a nice voice my mother had. I peeked out at the audience again. I could see everyone was listening and that they really liked her. And I remembered what Dad said in September, when Mom began her campaign. "She's just what this town of Cranberry Falls needs."

I ducked back and leaned against the curtain. I was scared. What if Mom won? She'd belong to all those people out there and never be home. We'd be eating Allison's hot dogs every night. And Willie would probably have a nervous breakdown with the telephone always ringing. Nobody would have time to talk to one another, and we'd never be a family again. I started to wish I'd never heard of politics or power lines or Mayor Quinn!

Mom was saying something about organizing a delegation to go to Washington to stop the overhead high-tension wires. The audience began applauding. They clapped so much she had to stop them so she could finish her speech.

Mr. Jessup was squirming in his chair. He lit his cigar.

Then Mayor Quinn spoke. I couldn't believe it, he sounded so awful. But then I couldn't believe myself because, deep down, I almost wished he sounded better so that he'd be sure to win, instead of my Mom. He was saying the power lines might be a rumor. Someone from the audience hollered, "Don't you wish, Myron!" The mayor began to perspire. Mr. Jessup squirmed some more and puffed on his cigar.

I knew Mayor Quinn was stalling. I watched him take a big red-checkered handkerchief out of his pocket and wipe his face. He muttered something into the mike about it being a little warm. Mrs. Duby nodded and looked around. She spotted the fan offstage behind me and motioned for me to turn it on.

I pulled the chain. The fan worked fine. It blew

Mr. Jessup's cigar smoke right in Mayor Quinn's face.

The mayor thanked Mrs. Duby and continued. Even with a microphone, the mayor sounded high and squeaky. With the fan going, you could barely hear him. And when someone from the audience shouted, "What did you say, Myron?" Mrs. Duby motioned for me to turn off the fan.

I pulled the chain again. It was like a windstorm. The fan went faster and louder. Papers began flying around the stage. Mrs. Duby frowned and shook her head at me. I gave the chain another yank.

The windstorm turned into a tornado. Jon said later it must have been a three-way switch. I looked over toward Mrs. Duby to see what I should do next. But she wasn't looking at me. She was staring at the mayor. And so was everyone else. His hair was gone. The fan had blown so hard, it took his hair right off! It was sailing up to the balcony.

"It's a wig!" someone gasped.

"No, it's a toupee," a lady said out front.

"It's a bush," I whispered to myself as I watched it spin around and around.

Suddenly it fell, right in some lady's lap. She was so startled she screamed and threw it back up in the air. This time it landed in the aisle someplace.

"WIN OR LOSE . . ."

No one moved. They were spellbound. They sat there watching Mayor Quinn. The mayor was touching his shiny bald head as if, like us, he noticed for the first time he was bald.

"Turn off that fan," Mr. Spano was yelling at me.

I didn't dare take any more chances. I pulled out the plug as fast as I could.

I heard a little boy say, "It's a Frisbee, Mommy," and the wig came flying back onto the stage. It landed under the table.

"Of all the dirty tricks," muttered Mr. Spano. He jumped out of his seat and grabbed the mayor and his hair and took them both off the stage.

The Republicans hurried after them.

People from the audience rushed up on the stage and congratulated Mom and the Democrats. Charlie Knots and Mr. Jessup were standing in a daze down near the footlights. They were as shocked as the rest of the crowd.

Allison and the boys ran over to the fan where I was. Allison began dancing all over the place. And the boys were trying not to laugh.

Ethan was practically jumping up and down. "She's going to win," he said. "She's going to win."

Then Kyle and Jon burst out laughing.

"Is it true?" I asked Jon. "Is Mom going to win?"

And that's when he said it. "Mom's going to win or lose by a hair, B.J." Then he began laughing again.

Allison twirled around and said, "Imagine, my mother the mayor."

I still couldn't believe it. "Maybe," I said.

Nancy saw me and hurried over. "Where were you? And guess what? I talked Tony Spano out of selling the newspaper with your picture in it."

"You didn't!"

"Yup. But I had to promise him we'd help scrape the bumper stickers off the windows tomorrow."

Flashbulbs were popping. It was Cyrilla Cornsby. She was up on the stage taking everyone's picture. And I knew she was looking for Mayor Quinn so that she could get the scoop of her life. I could see the headlines already: **Mayor Quinn, Bald as an Egg, Throws Toupee into Political Ring.**

She walked right up to me. "Have you seen Mayor Quinn, B.J.?"

I'd seen him all right. He was way over on the other side of the stage in a corner, trying to get his wig on straight.

I started to point over there, but somehow my arm went the other way. "He left." I was pointing to the back of the auditorium. "If you hurry, you might find him someplace in the parking lot."

Cyrilla flew down the stage steps, up the aisle, and out of the school.

I looked over at the mayor again. He was standing all alone in the corner. His red-checkered handkerchief was on top of his head, and he looked like he was crying in his toupee.

Suddenly I wanted to tell him it was all right—he looked okay bald.

And that's when I knew Dad was right. Mayor Quinn wasn't a bad guy at all. Nobody could look that sad and be a bad guy. The truth was, without that phony wig, he almost looked like a good guy.

★ ★ 14 ★ ★

"...by a Hair"

IT WAS ELECTION DAY. And it was pouring. Dad said that was a good sign for the Democrats because it would keep the Republicans at home. I asked him why it wouldn't keep the Democrats at home, too. He wasn't sure. "It's what the newscasters always say," he told me. I thought maybe I'd ask Mr. Shattelles in school tomorrow. But then I promised myself if I lived through the election today, I would never mention politics again.

The family was in a good mood, all except me. I wasn't. They were optimistic, but I kept seeing those faces in the auditorium at that big meeting when

Mayor Quinn lost his hair. They may have laughed, but they felt sorry for him. And I had a feeling they were going to vote for him.

Cranberry Falls is divided into eight election districts. We'd all learned that when we started campaigning for Mom. And Mom had explained that the election results would come in from the committeemen in each district over the telephones at headquarters. Since the day headquarters opened, we knew that was where we'd all be on election night.

"When will we know?" asked Jon.

"Well, the polls close at nine," Dad said. "The poll workers go to the back of the voting machines and read the results to the committeemen. Then the committeemen phone the results in to their headquarters. We should know by about nine-thirty."

"You mean, everyone telephones the railroad station?" said Allison.

"Just the Democratic committeemen, stupid," said Ethan.

"The Republican committeemen telephone their own headquarters across the street," explained Kyle.

"And then we'll know who the mayor is?" I asked.

"Then we'll know who the mayor is," said Mom.

Nobody said anything else. We didn't have to. We were all thinking the same thing. Would Mom win?

Later in the afternoon, it stopped raining and

Mom and Dad went out to vote. When they came back, Mom said we should all rest because we'd be staying up so late.

I "rested" downstairs in the keeping room, working on the scrapbook, my P.R. present for Mom.

I hadn't realized I'd practically filled it. There were only a couple of pages left. Mom could finish it tomorrow, with the election results.

I glanced at the old clock on the wall. It was almost seven. We'd forgotten to have dinner. It didn't matter. Nobody was hungry anyway. The phone was suddenly so quiet, nothing seemed normal except the ticking of the clock. Even Willie had given up. He'd fallen asleep under the kitchen desk, waiting for the telephone to ring.

"Better get dressed, B.J.," Mom called down.

I took the scrapbook upstairs and hid it under my pillow. I could hear Ethan grumbling about wearing a shirt and tie.

"Cyrilla will want a picture of the whole family, I'll bet," said Allison.

My stomach felt a little funny, and when Allison mentioned we'd better have some hot dogs or something before we left, it felt terrible.

We drove down Main Street. It was deserted, and as quiet as the keeping room. But I'd never seen so many cars. They were parked on both sides of the street. It looked like half the town was in front of the Republican headquarters and the other half was parked around the railroad station.

"Congratulations, Dorothy," Dad said as he parked the car. "This is the first time in a quarter of a century that the Democrats have had more than two cars at their headquarters on election night." He gave Mom a big kiss. "No matter what happens, you've already accomplished something."

"You kept the two-party system alive, Mom," said Kyle.

"She brought it back to life, you mean," Ethan told him.

The Christmas lights were lit up all over the station house. Mr. Grove had attached huge floodlights on the big maple tree. It was as bright as day.

We must have been the last to arrive because everyone else was already there. Sam Jessup and Charlie Knots hurried over and pretended to be friendly. They even had the nerve to wish Mom luck. Cyrilla was running back and forth across the street, talking to the candidates.

Earlier, Kyle had put the platform back up in front of the station because the Mudheads were coming to help celebrate after Mom won.

Right now, Ethel Grove was standing on the

platform next to a tremendous blackboard. Joe Belluci was running in and out of the station, checking on the phones.

"All these people would never fit in the tiny waiting room," Dad said. "Ethel will put the results on the blackboard out here as the districts call in. That way, we can keep track of how things are going."

I decided to stay with Jon. He'd be better than a pocket calculator when it came to adding up the votes. They'd come in fast, and it would be close. We knew that.

The clock at Town Hall struck nine. The polls were closed. Suddenly it was so quiet, you'd think we were in church. And I'll bet they were all praying the Democrats would win, at least on the railroad side of the street.

It seemed like we waited hours instead of minutes for the first call. When the phone rang, Joe Belluci ran into the waiting room. "It's District Two, on the north side of town," he shouted at the doorway. "Pinkerton, 260 votes . . . Quinn, 244."

Everyone cheered.

The Republican headquarters were getting calls now, too. I could see Tony Spano in the window across the street, biting his nails.

I didn't blame him. It was going to be so close, I didn't think I could stand it. But the telephone was ringing again, and this time Mr. Grove was inside, answering and hollering out to his wife, Ethel. "It's District Four. Pinkerton, 201 votes . . . Quinn, 239."

"Ohhh." The crowd was disappointed.

Mom and Dad were up on the platform with Ethel Grove. Mom saw me and winked. I gave her an okay sign for encouragement.

Before I could look over and see how Tony was doing, the telephone rang again.

Belluci hollered the numbers out. He was pretty excited. "It's District Five. Pinkerton, 245 votes . . . Quinn, 225."

"Yea, that's the way to go, Dorothy," someone yelled back in the crowd.

"What does that make it, Jon?" I asked.

"Quiet," he said. "Mr. Grove has another call."

"It's District Six, on the other side of town," he shouted. "Pinkerton, 278 votes . . . Quinn, 170."

The crowd cheered again and began laughing.

"That makes it, Pinkerton, 984 votes and Quinn, 878," said Jon.

Allison was standing on the other side of him. "She's going to win. I knew it all along."

MY MOTHER THE MAYOR, MAYBE

"Don't be too sure," Jon said. "There's four districts left, and they're big ones. Anything can happen."

The telephones were all ringing. Cyrilla Cornsby kept running back and forth. You could tell who was ahead by where Cyrilla was. Right now, she was on our side of the street.

"District One is in," Joe yelled. He didn't sound so happy. "Pinkerton, 200 votes . . . Quinn, 350."

"No!" moaned the crowd.

"Mom's behind," Jon told me. I knew that. Cyrilla was going back to the Republican headquarters and that Spano character was grinning like a monkey.

But then Mr. Grove was saying, "Hooray, it's Pinkerton, 379 votes . . . Quinn, 285. That's District Eight. And I've got District Seven too. Pinkerton, 298 votes . . . Quinn, 266!"

"Those are the districts where we campaigned," shouted Kyle.

Ethan was hopping around and not saying anything, but he had his fingers crossed. Up on the platform, Mom and Dad were hugging each other. The Mudheads began setting up their music stands, and Cyrilla was running back over to our side.

I couldn't believe it. My mother was going to be the next mayor of Cranberry Falls!

It was District Three that did it. That was the one section of town the power lines wouldn't be going through. And, like Mom said, if something doesn't affect you personally, you just don't care.

Joe Belluci cried when he hollered, "It's District Three and it isn't good. Pinkerton, 199 votes . . . Quinn, 342."

As long as it didn't affect them, District Three didn't care if the power lines passed through the rest of Cranberry Falls. Mayor Quinn won District Three by a landslide, and he won the election by 61 votes.

"Mom lost," Jon whispered as Cyrilla dashed back to the Republicans. "Final results, Pinkerton, 2060 votes . . . Quinn, 2121."

Almost everyone was crying. I couldn't see Mom. There were too many people crowding around her. Allison was biting her lip and trying not to cry. The boys were looking pretty sad.

Ethel Grove was the only Democrat who won, and she was crying more than anybody because she didn't want to be town clerk at all. "I can't even type," she wept. "Mr. Jessup promised me if I ran, I wouldn't win."

Across the street at the Republican headquarters, I could see the camera bulbs flashing through the store windows. Nobody was crying over there, I'll bet.

I felt really sick to my stomach. I had to go behind

the maple tree and throw up. It was Allison who found me.

"It was those hot dogs," she said and put her arm around me.

"It was politics," I told her.

"Come on, B.J." She took my arm. "Mom says we have to go over to the Republican headquarters."

"What?" I pulled away. "So Tony Spano can laugh at us? Never."

"We have to, B.J. The whole family."

"Sure, so Cyrilla can take a family portrait." I sneered.

"No." She looked right at me. "So everyone will know we're good sports."

I followed the family across the street.

Cyrilla tried to get everyone in the picture. Maybe Mom will put it in the back of my scrapbook with the election results. At least Mom doesn't look like Mayor Quinn anymore. And he looks happy, even without his hair. And Allison finally made it, right in the center. If I'd known I'd have to stand next to Tony Spano, I never would have gone across the street and into the Republican headquarters. I don't care who thinks I'm a bad sport.

★ ★ 15 ★ ★

The Telephone Call

WHEN WE GOT HOME, I went straight to my room to get Mom's scrapbook—and to think. Mom thought I was upset on account of the election. I didn't know whether I was or not. I must say, though, it was nice to have a mother come into my bedroom and talk.

"Things don't always work out the way you want them to, B.J., but most of the time, things work out for the best."

I didn't say anything.

"We're still a family."

"But you wanted to be the first woman mayor of Cranberry Falls, and you might have been if it wasn't for me."

"If it wasn't for you?"

"All those awful publicity things."

"Awful? Why, they were wonderful. I got more votes than any Democrat in Cranberry Falls ever has, and in a couple of years, you might have another chance to be a P.R. person."

"Huh?"

"Maybe I'll run again."

I took a deep breath. "I don't know if I want you to be a mayor. I want you to, and I don't want you to."

Mom hugged me. "Well, we've got plenty of time to think about it."

I pulled the scrapbook out from under my pillow and gave it to her.

"It's beautiful," sighed Mom. She flipped through the pages. "And I'll keep it forever. B.J. Pinkerton, you are the best P.R. person."

"You sound like Nancy."

"I mean it," Mom said. "No wonder I almost won. The Pinkertons made the newspaper every day."

"But all that work for nothing."

"B.J. Pinkerton." Mom sat down at the foot of my

bed. "What a thing to say. We've all grown and are better people because of everything politics has made us aware of. And you, you've progressed more than anyone. And that's what life is about, growing and getting to be a better person. Come on, now. Get fixed up. I've invited the volunteers and some friends over to celebrate."

"Celebrate? But we lost."

"We lost and we won, too! The power lines won't go through—we've got enough people on our side to stop them. Love still has her lower field, and because of your petition, the mayor's realized the old zoning law is no longer practical. From now on, if you want a horse, you only need three acres, like in Middleview. You see, B.J., when you start getting involved and caring, you *can* change things. Politics gives you the chance to change things and make them better."

"The Democrats still lost!"

"But they came closer to winning than ever before. Maybe next time they'll win."

"And what about Jessup and Knots?"

"I really don't know, B.J. You can change things. But you can't always change people. There are always people like Jessup and Knots—"

"And Tony Spano," I added.

Mom smiled. "They're not such bad guys. Most of

the time they're not worth worrying about. Eventually, they turn into good guys."

"You hope," I said. "But you could have *won* the election! What if they had—"

Mom interrupted me. "No 'what ifs.' The election is over. And I'm proud that each member of this family has devoted a little time to public service."

"Like your dad said we should!"

Mom got up. "Comb your hair. The Spanos will be dropping by any minute."

"The Spanos? But they're on the wrong side."

Mom laughed. "They're not going to stay. They're on their way to a victory party. But, like your father says, 'Just because we belong to different political parties doesn't mean we can't be friends.' And we are friends."

Mom went downstairs.

I looked in the mirror and straightened the ribbon on my pigtail. The doorbell rang. Willie was barking like crazy, and I could hear all the Spanos talking and laughing.

"You may have progressed," I said to the face in the mirror. "And you may care about the whole world." I straightened the other ribbon. "But you haven't changed your mind at all. Just remember, B.J. Pinkerton, you still can't stand that Tony Spano."

THE TELEPHONE CALL

I ran downstairs.

They were all in the kitchen.

"Hi, B.J."

"Hi, Tony." What a jerk!

The telephone rang, and Willie began turning around in circles near the desk. Things were getting back to normal.

"I'll get it, Mom." I picked up the receiver. "This is B.J. Pinkerton. Who's calling, please?"

"The governor."

I nearly dropped the phone. If Tony Spano hadn't been in the same room, I'd have sworn someone was playing a trick on me.

"I've just heard the Cranberry Falls election results on the radio," the governor continued, "and I'd like to speak to Dorothy Pinkerton."

I held my hand over the mouth of the receiver and yelled, real loud, so Tony Spano and the whole town could hear. "It's the governor calling Mom."

As they all crowded around, I handed Mom the phone.

"The governor?" whispered Allison. "Darn. Why couldn't I have answered the telephone?"

"Shh," Dad said.

We listened, but nothing made much sense until Mom hung up.

"I've been appointed by the governor to head a

committee. We're going to study the possibility of putting all power lines underground in the future. Not only for Cranberry Falls, but for the whole state," she explained. "And then, we're going to Washington to present our report to the Federal Power Commission!" Mom was so excited, she was crying. "The governor said he was watching my campaign and"—Mom looked right at me—"he liked my publicity. He's sure I can handle the job."

Dad picked up Mom and set her on the kitchen counter. The boys started singing, "For She's a Jolly Good Fellow." Allison and I yelled, "Speech! Speech!" The Spanos thought we were all crazy, but we didn't care.

Allison began twirling around. "Imagine, my mother the governor, someday."

"Could be!" I said.

The Last Picture

THE NEXT DAY, at school, Nancy was wearing a black armband. She said she was in mourning because of the election results.

"But tell your mother, my father says it's just as well. He heard there are mice in Town Hall."

"I hope they're in Mr. Jessup's office," I said.

"He's in Town Hall?"

"Only as dogcatcher. Those two never fooled Mayor Quinn at all."

"What happened to that other guy?"

"Charlie Knots? Since he found out Sam Jessup

made a mistake, he's not speaking to anybody. His property wasn't anywhere near where they planned to put the power lines!"

We were in social studies when Cyrilla Cornsby arrived to take a human-interest picture for the *Courier* of me and Tony Spano shaking hands. How can it be a human-interest picture when Tony Spano isn't even human?

I asked Cyrilla if Nancy could be in the picture too, because she helped with the campaign. So Cyrilla asked the three of us to stand up near the blackboard with Mr. Shattelles.

Then, before she took the picture, Cyrilla presented me with a certificate from the newspaper. It's the one I'm holding in front of me that says *Outstanding Campaigner.* Tony Spano was so jealous, he had to run back to his desk and put on his stupid **Win with Quinn** hat.

I know it looks like it's Nancy I'm shaking hands with instead of Tony Spano. In fact, you can't see Tony Spano. Nancy was standing behind him and accidentally knocked off his hat. She caught it as it fell in front of his face, and that's when Cyrilla snapped the picture. It looks like Nancy's face is Tony's because his face is behind the stupid hat.

Anyway, that's me, and Tony, and Mr. Shattelles, and my friend Nancy.

CRANBERRY FALLS LOVES MAYOR QUINN, BUT NEXT TIME MS PINKERTONS GOING TO WIN!

OUTSTANDING CAMPAIGNER

Political Activists Are Honored

I forgot to ask her when she had time to write on the blackboard behind us.

After she took the picture, Cyrilla gave me a big hug. She said she got promoted out of the society column all because of me and my unusual P.R. work. They were putting her in the foreign news department.

Mr. Shattelles put us right to work. He said our assignment for next month would be career opportunities. Before the bell rang, we had to write a whole page on what careers we were interested in.

Going home on the bus, Nancy asked me what I wrote.

"Don't laugh," I said, "but I've been thinking. Women are going to be very important in shaping events in the world, Nancy. And someday I think I'll run for President."

"Don't laugh," Nancy said. "I wrote, I want to be a P.R. person, even if politics *is* a rough game."

"I'm not laughing, Nancy."

The bus stopped.

Mike Callahan was staring in the mirror at us. "Isn't there someone on this bus who gets off here?"

Nancy jumped up and headed out the door.

"You'll be the best P.R. person," I hollered out the window.

THE LAST PICTURE

That Nancy's crazy sometimes, but she's my best friend.

As the bus drove down the road, I could hear her yelling. And I'll bet all of Cranberry Falls could hear her too. "And you'll make the best President ever, B.J. Pinkerton!"

About the author

Pat Kibbe graduated from the American Academy of
Dramatic Arts, and besides Broadway, television,
and radio shows to her credit, she has also done
commercials for Perdue Chickens and Ruffles Potato
Chips. For her books, she draws from her own life.
The Pinkerton family in MY MOTHER THE MAYOR,
MAYBE bears a strong resemblance to her own
husband, dog, and five children (now grown).
Currently, Pat Kibbe and her husband live in
Yorktown Heights, N.Y. Her first book, THE
HOCUS-POCUS DILEMMA is also available in an
Apple Paperback edition from Scholastic, Inc.